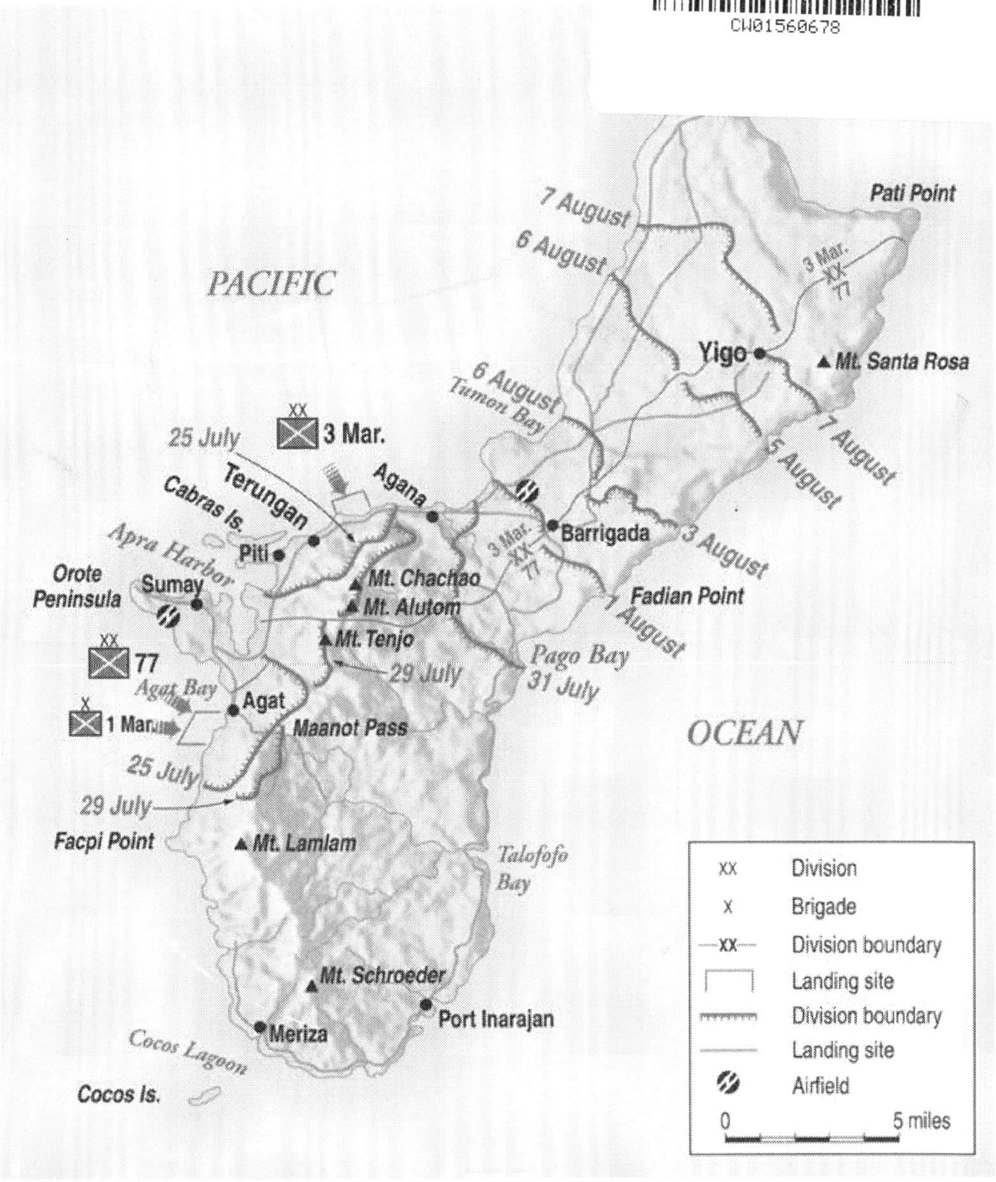

Pati Point

7 August

6 August

3 Mar.
XX
77

PACIFIC

Yigo ● ▲ *Mt. Santa Rosa*

6 August
Tumon Bay

7 August

25 July   XX ✕ 3 Mar.

Terungan

5 August

Cabras Is.   *Agana*

Apra Harbor   Piti ●   3 Mar.
XX
77   ● Barrigada   *3 August*

Orote
Peninsula   Sumay   ▲ *Mt. Chachao*   *Fadian Point*

▲ *Mt. Alutom*   *7 August*

XX ✕ 77   ▲ *Mt. Tenjo*

Agat Bay   ● Agat   *29 July*   *Pago Bay*
31 July

X ✕ 1 Mar.   *Maanot Pass*

25 July   OCEAN

29 July

Facpi Point   ▲ *Mt. Lamlam*   *Talofofo*
Bay

XX	Division
x	Brigade
----XX----	Division boundary
☐	Landing site
﹏﹏	Division boundary
───	Landing site
🌀	Airfield

▲ *Mt. Schroeder*

Cocos Lagoon   ● Meriza   ● Port Inarajan

Cocos Is.

0   5 miles

25 MARINE WAR DOGS GAVE THEIR LIVES LIBERATING GUAM IN 1944. THEY SERVED AS SENTRIES, MESSENGERS, SCOUTS. THEY EXPLORED CAVES, DETECTED MINES AND BOOBY TRAPS. SEMPER FIDELIS

KURT YONNIE KOKO BUNKIE
SKIPPER PONCHO TUBBY HOBO
NIG PRINCE FRITZ EMMY
MISSY CAPPY DUKE MAX
BLITZ ARNO SILVER BROCKIE
BURSCH PEPPER LUDWIG RICKEY
TAM (BURIED AT SEA OFF ASAN POINT)

GIVEN IN THEIR MEMORY AND ON BEHALF OF THE SURVIVING MEN OF THE 2nd AND 3rd MARINE WAR DOG PLATOONS, MANY OF WHOM OWE THEIR LIVES TO THE BRAVERY AND SACRIFICE OF THESE GALLANT ANIMALS
BY WILLIAM W. PUTNEY DVM C.O. 3rd DOG PLATOON
DEDICATED THIS DAY 21 JULY 1994

I clutched my Thompson Submachine gun tight in my sweaty hands while I crouched low in the brutal jungle terrain with my finger on the trigger of the powerful and sturdy weapon. As I looked ahead about twenty yards to Cerberus who was on point, he paused for a moment encompassed in thick vines to sniff the breeze with his snout high in the air. The sleek Doberman Pinscher was becoming more cautious and I felt the tension rise in my chest as I could feel the presence of the enemy through him. We crept up between the broad ferns soaked in droplets of humid condensation, wading through the dense foliage all around us on edge. My Platoon Sergeant had sent us ahead by ourselves as advanced scouts behind enemy lines, and I knew the immense danger of this mission, we were surrounded by a blood thirsty and desperate Japanese army with absolutely no backup. A few units had been decimated by a machine gun nest or two with only a few survivors the day before, and today we lost radio contact with another squad several hours ago with no signs of what had happened.

My superiors pulled the Platoon back, they weren't willing to advance and take any more losses on this hostile ridge of Mount Santa Rosa until they knew the situation up ahead and what we were up against. I had actually come across the carnage and aftermath of that unfortunate encounter about seventy yards back towards the southeast. I found the bodies of my fellow soldiers mutilated in a small clearing, their blood splashed against the hanging canopy and thick burgundy puddles collected on the muddy ground. Small trees as well as human bodies had been cut in half from the potent heavy machine guns, the squad leader's head had been cleaved clean off his neck, his torso ransacked with heavy ammunition, his chest had nothing left to it but an unidentifiable hole of butchery. Cerberus had walked up to the nearest body and smelled the soldier, even nudging his hand with his nose, but the casualties were already long cold and lifeless. All eighteen bodies were there and accounted for, a severed hand strewn here, a bloody and bullet riddled helmet thrown there, but the weapons and supplies were missing, undoubtedly scavenged by the enemy. I read a set of dog tags that I picked up out of a pool of blood, they belonged to a kid I knew. I knelt next to him and placed the tags on his chest and closed his eyelids out of respect before looking away from his pale, bloated form. The flies hovered all around the nauseating foul stench as my countrymen paid the ultimate price, and I decided to move quickly out of the killzone and submerge back into the forest before I became the nineteenth confirmed loss.

The discovery had altered my course and I decided to trek straight west from the bloodbath and then commence going north again towards the direction from which the bullets seemed to have hailed. Cerberus had guided me expertly, as he effortlessly wove between trees and bushes smelling out the enemy that he could undeniably taste in the jungle air. I rested my weary legs as I leaned up against the wide trunk of a moss covered tree and listened for any discernable sound, from a twig snapping under the slightest amount of weight applied to it, to the more grim explosion of gunfire. After hearing nothing, we continued on our search and destroy mission, serenaded by the sounds of the tropical birds overhead in the branches and buzz of insects on the ground. We maneuvered in the thick vegetation a few more yards and then past a shallow stream that trickled under us and filled my boots with cool water. We slowly plodded on, parting our way through thick Tangan Tangan brush and made it a few more yards in jungle so dense and murky that we could barely see ten feet in front of us. That's when Cerberus halted in his silent stalking through the underbrush and alerted me to the machine gun nest that we were searching for. He signaled to it by turning his head to the right, motioning directly towards the astonishingly well camouflaged gun turret. But all the camouflage in the jungle couldn't hide them from the Doberman's superior senses, as I'm sure he could hear them breathing in the dug in hole and smell the nervous sweat that emanated from their pores in the tropical heat. The Japanese were sitting low behind a Type 92 Shiki Kikanju heavy machinegun, what we called a 'Woodpecker' because of the distinct stuttering noise it produced when firing. They had it dug down a few feet with sandbags forming a wall, concealing even more of the Woodpecker and the three men operating the deadly weapon. The sand bags had small bushes, tree branches, and palm leafs and ferns all protruding out between the crevices blending it perfectly into the background. The hundred and twenty pound old contraption of death was raised just above the sandbags on its tripod as the ribbed barrel poked out, pointing precariously close to our position.

As far as we knew, they hadn't spotted us yet, and I quickly rushed forward a few feet into a military crawl closer to my dog. The nest wasn't further than a hundred and fifty feet away, and if we were discovered, they would instantly obliterate us and the ground we stood on. Upon nearing Cerberus, I soundlessly commanded him to lay low to the ground while we observed the scenario through our trained reconnaissance in silence. After some intense minutes of laying in the bushes trying to get a read on the enemy, I could see the heavy machinegun was pointed just south of our position and had a hundred and fifty round metal strip loaded, feeding the instrument of destruction with 7.7 mm cartridges, one after another. Occasionally we would see the dull metal helmet of a soldier pop up and scan the terrain to the south with a set of worn binoculars, then duck back down with the others. It was excruciating to stay so close to the machine gun unit and in their direct path of fire and yet not be able to get a clean shot at any of them, still we had the element of surprise. Furthermore, if we were to so much as move a muscle and make any kind of noise, it would be the last move we ever made. My dog made a sign to his left, pointing with his wedge shaped head in the opposite direction of where all my attention was focused, and I told him in the slightest of whispers, 'Relax, stay boy.' I had adrenaline pulsating through my veins and a uneasiness bubbling up in my stomach while my heart pounded at a rapidly rising rate, meanwhile Cerberus seemed as calm as ever, trusting his life in me as much as I trusted mine in him.

After much internal debate while lying in the thick and thorny underbrush trying so diligently not to rustle a leaf or even breathe too loudly, I made the dangerous decision to close the gap and maneuver for a better attack. My loyal Doberman and I stalked through the Mulberry thickets and underbrush in a stealthy crawl, the pace wasn't faster than a tortoise and every muscle was so rigid and stiff that my joints ached as I overthought the placement of every forearm and knee on the cluttered forest floor. At about 50 feet away, I placed us in some fern patches near a grove of Coconut palms and felt it prudent to use an MK2 Pineapple Grenade, ready to try and lob it over their makeshift bunker walls and then rush them after the explosion. I ever so cautiously moved my hand down to my belt and unclipped one of the Grenades, however as I rolled to my side and positioned myself to throw it, Cerberus snapped his head back to the left at full attention now. I looked back to that direction in-between his sleek black triangular ears, and after a minute or two I could see a line of Japanese infantry approaching right towards our position, maybe a hundred and twenty feet away on their way to the machine gun nest as reinforcements most likely. I pointed at the ground harshly, telling the dog to lay back down and tried to count the number of closing enemies. It was more than four, then I counted seven, then ten came into view, finally I counted all eleven closing in from forty feet away. I was shocked, my entire plan ruined as the line of armed men drew ever closer through the bushes and trees.

I couldn't move or try to run, I wouldn't make it two steps before being ripped apart from all sides now. I asked myself if we should lay as still as conceivable and pray they walked past us carelessly and fail to take notice? Should I hope they didn't step right on us as they neared to twenty feet and continued right for us? The men at the machine gun turret started to talk in their foreign tongue as they too took notice of their incoming comrades. I could feel my lungs begin to hyperventilate as my options were all but none at this point. My Doberman stared at me with his intense dark eyes looking for direction, my hands were clammy and my thoughts tended to revert back to running. I didn't see a way out of it for us, and now was the moment of truth in the midst of the enemy's angry hordes. I snapped, realizing that I was most probably going to die, and in which case I would go down shooting and try and take as many of these mother fuckers with me as I could. I yanked the pin out of the MK2 and tossed it hard with my right arm as it descended with perfect trajectory and landed on the flat surface of the machine gun nest's sandbag wall. It fortuitously bounced off the bag and fell into the hole, clanking around off the Woodpecker with metal clangs as they quickly realized something was wrong and frantically scampered around looking for what it was.

In that awkward moment that it took for the three operators in the nest to realize the foreign green object that fell between them was a live Grenade, valuable seconds were already eaten away. I came up from the bushes in one fluid motion with my M1928 Thompson's wooden butt stock pressed securely against my shoulder and gripping hard on the wood grain rear grip as I pressed down on the trigger. My submachine gun burst a violent spray of lead as I laced the nearest soldiers in the line with .45 ACP rounds and chopped them down one by one as the blow back action unleashed a fully automatic doom that ripped them apart. The first few fell in a blood soaked pile before they could raise their weapons, although they did take the initial brunt of my attack and allowed the rear soldiers to become aware of my presence as they raised their rifles and carbines. I persisted on and held tight to the wooden fore grip, concentrating on holding the recoiling weapon down to keep the barrel from rising as I rained full metal jackets down on the frightened soldiers as they took aim upon me. My dog laid at my feet still in the bushes as the Tommy gun's 50 round drum magazine was feeding the powerful submachine gun the man stopping rounds while I began sweeping the weapon left to right and watching the scorching projectiles slice through the flesh of the closest men while hot brass casing streamed to my side.

Just then the Pineapple Grenade I had thrown on the machinegun nest rocked the earth with a deafening explosion as the two ounces of compacted TNT wrapped in iron was detonated by the time delayed percussion cap. The simplistic fragmentation bomb wreaked havoc in the form of sharp twisted iron shrapnel as the MK2 Frag Grenade tore the Woodpecker operators into mincemeat with chunks of singeing hot metal exploding throughout the nest and shredding the soldiers to bloody chunks of corpses while simultaneously sabotaging the Type 92 Shiki Kikanju into useless flaming wreckage. I continued to lay down suppressing fire on the procession of men now shooting back while running for cover, hitting one Japanese soldier in the neck and watching as the blood erupted from his carotid artery, spraying a fine red mist from his throat as he fell to the jungle floor, rolling and clutching at his fatal wound. I let off the trigger momentarily while I aimed to the right and towards a few of the infantry men that were dispersing in that direction, and pressed hard on the kill switch again. My Thompson raged and recoiled as spent shell casings were ejected on the left of the weapon and the bullets sank into the soldiers in front of me, ripping the life from the surprised men as they painfully crumpled. Now as I focused my aim back to the left, I was struck with a round in the side of my torso by a well-placed shot from a bayonetted Type 38 Arisaka, and my reality quickly fell back to the hell that I was in. The lethal projectile had sliced clean through me and exited out of my back as it devastated my right side and sent shock waves of pain throughout my body like sharp lightning bolts of molten lead.

I somehow managed to stand through the excruciating pain while my blood flowed like warm rivers from an entry and exit wound that sent shivers of anxiety as well as agony down my spine. I refused to let up, and turned my weapon on the soldier kneeling down about twenty yards away behind a fallen log. He was ejecting a round from his bolt action rifle and reloading when I squeezed off a couple rounds that delivered retribution into the man's chest up to his face, deforming his excited expression into a gory monstrosity as his face caved in on itself from the burst of machinegun fire. His remaining comrades gathered behind the fallen ancient tree covered in green moss and flowering, thorny vines next to my latest kill and hunkered down for cover. My clip was running low I knew, so I utilized the last remaining rounds in rapid burst of suppressive fire as I lowered down to one knee and reached for a fresh box clip.

Before I had time to reach for the new clip and release the spent drum, I was struck hard in the shoulder and leveled to the ground on my back by the force, falling into the brush next to my dog. One of the enemy footsoldiers had let off a stream of lead from his Type 99 LMG, and now blood spurted and surged from the new gouging wound as the pain burned through my mind. The rest followed suit and unloaded their Japanese Garands and Light Machineguns as the thick bushes that covered Cerberus and I were exploding all around us. I struggled knowing we had no other choice but to fight through the intensifying pain, and released the drum and slapped a fresh clip into my trusty Trenchsweeper. I seen the Japanese squad send two soldiers to the right to flank me while the other four stayed hidden behind the old log covered in damp green moss and slithering vines. They continued shooting unceasingly, pinning us down in the brush with their friends encroaching on our side to finish us off. I reached for my last MK2 Grenade, pulled the pin and held it for a few seconds regarding the live explosive as the fuse ticked away with my blood trickling down my arm and slowly accumulating on the dark green device packed full of TNT. Then I launched it using all my dwindling strength with perhaps no more than a second remaining on the Grenade and it exploded in midair directly over their position as the shrapnel ripped apart the soldiers in a thunderous explosion of hell, leaving the log covered in dead bodies tossed like rag dolls from the immense concussion force.

This victory was short lived though as the throwing of the Grenade had exposed my position with my arm above the bushes and the last two soldiers charged us with their bayonets pointed and rifles firing. Cerberus was hit first as he courageously stood up in front of me, absorbing the lethal shot that dropped him back to the ground. With the two infantry in a full out sprint and within steps of us, ready to plunge the brutal blades at the ends of their rifles into our vital organs, I raised up the Tommy gun with my ears ringing and shot the first man square in the eye as half his face and head exploded in the violent process of collecting a few more of the rounds at close range in my defiant automatic burst. His counterpart had taken the opportunity to fire point blank now completely on top of me, yet his shot smashed into the Thompson with a turbulent force that bent the receiver, smashing the weapon out of my hands as the submachine gun miraculously caught the rifle cartridge. Undeterred, the soldier took the remaining two steps towards me with his rifle raised like a spear and came down with all his might, holding the rifle in two hands and driving the blade towards my stomach for the finishing blow.

Out of nowhere, Cerberus rushed from my side and leapt towards the bloodthirsty, insatiable warrior and intercepted the deadly stab at the last second, closing his long snout around the man's left arm in midair and sinking his ivory sickle teeth deep into his flesh. The Doberman latched on and yanked the man's momentum sideways as he dragged his arm with his insanely powerful jaws and muscular mass. Cerberus' valiant act caused the scalpel sharp bayonet blade to narrowly miss my abdomen that was already gushing blood from one of the nasty bullet wounds, and now Cerberus was crushing the Japanese soldier's arm in his overpowering grip, wrenching the man side to side as the Doberman pulled him to the ground. Cerberus kept ripping at the Hetai while he savagely shook back and forth, gnawing on the man's flailing arm as he screamed. I took the chance in all the turmoil and un-holstered my 1911 Colt and as the man fought back against the wounded dog latched onto his bloody arm and reached for his blade, I fired a .45 caliber round from my back, placing the lead projectile directly into the temple of the erratic soldier as his body went still after the earsplitting sound, and he dropped to the ground a half second later, swallowed by the bushes beside us.

Cerberus finally released the last soldier's torn up arm from his predatorial jaws and trotted over to me through a limp, where I laid bleeding out from the awful wounds inflicted during the skirmish. I scanned over my dog, and found the fur on his back was soaked with warm, sticky blood. I then began to pet the shiny black canine who panted his bad breathe next to my face and refused to recognize the pain or the wound itself. I rubbed his ear and told him, 'You're going to get a medal of valor for this, and a purple heart. You'll be going home boy, a hero, and gunna be having puppies and telling everybody about your master… Right boy?' The Doberman continued to nuzzle me with his big nose and I realized that this was where I would die, in the Guam Jungle on the other side of the world. I would be a hero though, taking out a hidden machine gun nest and a squad of soldiers with me, can't say that wasn't a hell of a way to go out fighting. Cerberus looked at my face with pure loyalty in his dark brown eyes and I could feel my strength draining with the gross amounts of blood that were hemorrhaging from my injuries. I knew death was closing in on me, and that was fine, I was a soldier. I had accepted this close proximity of death with my duty a long time ago, but as it drew closer, my recent endeavors in this war began to flash back over me, as my vision faded to the vivid memories of war.

Chapter 1

Our travels from the nearest friendly tropical island in the South Pacific had left some of my comrades seasick as they struggled to control their vomiting through the rough ocean waters to the hostile island of Guam. It was July, 21st 1944, we had recently been briefed on the campaign before departure, about the carpet bombing raids by our B-25's in the prior weeks and the Battleships more recent close bombardment meant to soften up the Japanese defenses. The Navy had even sent in underwater demolition teams from July 14th to the 17th to clear the invasion sights of all sunken obstacles and floating mines, and this specialized Platoon fully realized the gravity of the situation and that this would be the Marine War Dogs' first real test to prove our merit. Many of our superiors felt we were an oddity, a distinct liability and a kind of sideshow that most in the Marines thought was a complete waste of time and resources. Cerberus was calm at my side in our rocky world, his shiny jet black fur ran course through my fingers as I pet the Doberman's dark solid head, his huge pink tongue hung to the side with a panting rhythm in the stuffy steel cabin. The U.S.S. Sherman, our Navy transport vessel bounced and rolled in the waves as we neared the sandy beaches on the west side of the island. The first wave of troops had already battled through intense mortar and artillery fire during the landing and taken several hundred yards of beachhead, they were making slow and bloody gains in the interior jungle and hills. The Japanese were dug into fortified positions on cliffs and ridges, picking apart our advances with guerrilla warfare hit an runs as well as countless ambushes from sniper fire and heavy machineguns. Their regular forces held their lines fearlessly, even as our battleships' 14 inch guns blasted away, punishing the IJA positions with High Explosive rounds. It still didn't stop the Japanese from holding the ground, with 75 mm artillery hailing rounds back at the landing forces from protected and hidden bunkers in the cliffside. From the fields and hills their cumbersome 105's were hitting us hard in combination with every kind of Mortar they could direct, blasting our troops and landing craft in deadly explosions. It would be a long, drawn out affair with an abundance of casualties for our brothers in arms if something didn't change, and our unit of war dogs intended to be that very change.

It was a strange feeling as our transport ship neared the landing spot, a surreal sense of awe kind of enveloped me. The training Cerberus and I had accomplished during our 14 weeks together at Camp Lejeune was grueling and encompassing, but it was nothing compared to the real thing. We were about to step out into an all-out world war and go head on against the unforgiving hell of combat with a crazed, kamikaze extreme, enemy. No more exercises, no more dog training scenarios, this is where death and life were no more separated than mere milligrams of squeeze on a hairpin trigger, and we would definitely be in the crosshairs if we didn't keep our heads down and stay sharp.

We got the call from our Staff Sergeant and I looked down the line at the fellow handlers and their canines as we geared up and left the dimly lit, protective cabin and made our way out onto the main deck and into the overcast and windy sea air as a slight drizzle was showering down on us. There were two handlers to a dog, and each group of two men and their dog was specialized as either a scouting unit, messenger unit, or some just operated as sentry units for road checkpoints and forward bases yet to be established. Those Sentry dogs were meant to help the MP's on guard duty at day, but especially at night, as well as occupy fox holes on the front line so soldiers could sleep. The messenger dogs were specifically trained to run coded messages and supplies between one handler at a forward position back to the other handler, usually with the main forces away from the front line. This was an incredibly hazardous job as the daring canines ignored gunfire, mortar shells, and discharging explosions to deliver pivotal information that could turn the tide of battle and save countless lives. That's why we were here after all, to save American lives and bring freedom to the people of Guam. These messenger units would come in handy when we entered the jungle and the Japanese started cutting our radio wires and communication cables in the dense frontier of tropical forest and rugged mountains.

Then there was the scout unit class which I belonged to, an along with my friend, Lance Corporal Michael Blanchet, we were the handlers trained with our amazing and loyal Doberman Pinscher, Cerberus. We specialized as advanced reconnaissance for the Regiment, and with plenty of guerilla warfare expected from the tens of thousands of armed Japanese hiding all over the jungle terrain, we would see an abundance of action. The Japanese Army had orders from Emperor Hirohito to fight to the bitter end with no surrender, making these Scout Units indispensable to our Platoons. We would be on the front lines sniffing out snipers, clearing pill boxes and caves, and leading point on all advancing patrols. It was a dangerous job that I had been specially recruited for by a high ranking Marine Officer that I was connected to, nearly a year ago now. I wasn't much of a dog person back then but had become a distinguished marksman as a Sniper for the 2'nd Marine Division, my superiors took notice and selected me for further training in a highly classified sniper school. While enlisted in this program, I was contacted and told of a top secret an unprecedented experiment taking place by the Marines in which they were going to be combining soldiers and canines as cohesive working units to potentially accomplish things never before done on the battlefield. The Marine Officer felt I was the perfect candidate and captured my attention with his spiel of a U.S. War Dog Detachment in North Carolina, and as odd as it sounded to me, I had told him, 'Sign me up if it ever takes off, Sir.' How quickly the time had passed, now I felt inseparable from Cerberus and I was as enthusiastic about our first taste of action together as he was.

The rain shower seemed to be letting up as the sky continued to lighten while we prepared for the mission with haste. The units of dog men began climbing down the roped ladders hanging to the churning waters off the sides of the cold grey ship to the multiple waiting Landing Track Vehicles. After we made the descent with all our gear and weapons secured, the Dobermans were awkwardly lowered off the Sherman by ropes and harnesses the twenty or so feet down into the small LVT's. The waters and hard limestone coral reef around the island were too shallow for the bigger vessel to dock anywhere close to the shore, and it was much faster and more strategic to get our squads to the beaches with speed in staggered positions to where each War Dog unit would be deployed to different Platoons already in the midst of fighting. Fortunately the shoreline had already been cleared by the initial landing and our invasion had secured sizable beachheads at two points. Our briefing had illustrated a beach assault led by General Shepherd's 1'st Provisional Marine Brigade who would be joined later by the 77th Army Infantry just south of the Orote Peninsula next to the town of Agat. The second invasion point was headed by the 3'rd Marine Division at the Asan beach, where Major General Turnage was taking charge of the landing assault on the north side of the Orote Peninsula near Agana. My squad was being attached to this Division and we had strict orders for each unit to find our Company on the frontline as soon as possible and start leading the fight.

With the last of the Doberman Pinschers now only dangling feet from the amphibious assault vehicle that we referred to as the Gator or sometimes Amphtrack, we looked towards the chaotic beaches. Some of the men kissed the crosses that hung around their necks, others took one long, last look at pictures of their sweetheart back home in the States. I patted Cerberus on the neck and told the powerfully built dog, 'It's time boy. Here we go.' The last canine was released from the tethered harness and the Gator revved up its motors as we began closing the last few hundred yard expanse of tumbling waves to the island of Guam. We kept our heads low out of necessity as much as from our training as we watched LCI Gunboats launch 4.5 inch rockets that spiraled over our heads and descended upon the cliffs and hills with fiery detonations. The invasion had already been under way for a couple hours now and although we had lost over 20 LVT's on the initial assault landing, the beachfronts were well secured. However this didn't stop the IJA from blanketing the sea and beaches with unrelenting explosions from their artillery battalions at their strong points. The Japanese also used expertly coordinated heavy machinegun crossfire from Yona island and Bundschu ridge to decimate our advances, and in unerring combination with their fortified blockhouse at Guan Point whose Type 90 field guns roared, hurling devastating 75 mm rounds towards our Marines' every position. I had overheard an Officer on the ship galley tell someone over the radio that we had placed tanks on both the beaches by 0900 hours, and that relieved me somewhat knowing we had some armor support. I could see even from a distance the blood trails in the bombarded sand and corpses of my fallen comrades being piled together by the hundred. The massive 14 inch guns belched thunder from our Battleships behind us, offering artillery support to our forward lines immersed in tumultuous jungle warfare. Meanwhile the sea water would occasionally explode around us from a falling high explosive shell as the Imperial Japanese Army returned fire towards the invading forces as we pressed on through the hell. Our supply and support Marines were stacking up ammo dumps on the beaches and gathering our dead, as they awaited their body bags and coffins so they could make their final journey back home to be buried.

The amphibious boat hummed along cutting through the blue water as I noticed pieces of the sunken LVT's being manipulated by the tide, the surf crashing the floating portions along to the shore and pulling them back to sea in the perpetual foamy waves. From nearby in the water, I witnessed the torso of a man rolling on the crest of the wave towards the beach, missing limbs and bloated from the salty waters. I had heard stories of how bloodthirsty the Imperial Japanese Army could be, of the suicidal banzai attacks, and of their many sadistic executions where POW's heads were cleaved clean off by Samurai swords. Even with the constant eruptions of Japanese artillery blasting off through gun ports behind four foot thick concrete bunkers and the booming of our flotilla of battleships responding in turn, I could still hear my heartbeat in my eardrums, but I tried not to show it as I looked on to the ever nearing white sandy beaches. Most of the men and dogs looked tranquil, like the calm before the storm, a few others looked queasy, others were wired with anticipation as the Amphtrack bottomed out against the sandy island and the tracks under the boat kicked into gear with a whirling mechanical sound that jolted us forward the last remaining yards towards shore. I glanced to my left to witness the U-shaped cave command post carved into the sandstone cliffs hundreds of yards north, its heavy machineguns peppering the beaches and raining lead down on our positions. It was rumored by the men that Japanese General Takeshi Takashina himself was in those caves, commanding his forces while they fought to repel the invasion. As we hardened our faces, the gate crashed down and we started rushing the beaches with our rifles slung over our shoulders as we jogged towards the tree line. Two men to a sleek black Doberman dashed across the white sand in teams towards the trailheads. I jogged with Cerberus' leash in hand and Michael ran on the other side of the large dog as he bounded effortlessly ahead with our boots and paws churning up the blood stained sand as we avoided the deep craters left by artillery and bombs. After making it to the jungle, I looked at our squad around us, dogs panting while their triangular ears stood at attention, and soldiers checking for radio contact with our superiors. I could sense the trepidation in the squad, who could blame them, this was where we entered the war, and many of these guys were virgins to combat. We were trusting our lives in these dogs on top of it all, but as I looked at Cerberus with his fierce and intelligent eyes scanning the dense foliage, I felt confident in this unprecedented experiment of man and beast, so I grasped my rifle and took the lead, plunging into the jungle as the squad fell in line behind me.

We navigated the living and breathing forest of ever thickening Coconut Palms, Indian Almonds, and Sabal Palmetto trees twisting into an interlaced webbing of flora. The Indian Almonds were a dry season deciduous tree that towered over the canopy with mushroom crowns, their tiers of broad waxy leaves spreading wide and casting shade as the Palmettos and Coconut Palms sprouted and burgeoned in every available space left, forming a secondary canopy of spikey palm fronds. The squad of soldiers and dogs were quickly enveloped by the tropical forest in its mixture of thousands of shades of greens while the sweat ran from our helmets and down around our faces in profuse streams. The steaming atmosphere was physically draining, especially while carrying the added pounds of gear and weapons, but that was the price to pay as an enlisted Marine. The dogs instantly went into work mode as they led us to our objective point through the wilderness with animalistic ease. Our squad of eighteen soldiers was divided into four messenger units, four scouting units, and one sentry unit, and we all had our predetermined orders of which company each unit was to be attached to. This led us to disperse as we neared the front lines with five units going south to rendezvous with their companies, leaving four units to fork north. The two messenger dog units and the other scout unit were on our six as we came upon the main force of our Company in one of the first bases on Guam. The Commanding Officer, First Lieutenant Dunham met us in a makeshift bunker freshly dug, it was filled with radio equipment and supplies as men unfolded a camouflaged tent awning over us where we stood. Lieutenant Dunham said in a burly voice, 'Welcome to Guam boys! We've been expecting you, right now there's some intense fighting with the IJA out there about a hundred an fifty meters to the east, our men were doing a hell of a job pushing forward but the Japs aren't budging in some spots. Stiff resistance, bastards are dug in, there's several areas like this that we've encountered, like Hill D and F. And god damn Chonito Ridge has already cost us a few hundred Marines for Christ sakes! The Fonte heights is another sector that has been impossible to gain a foothold on, and I'll be sending a War Dog Unit to each of the worst zones. We started losing heavy casualties in the last hour and progress is slowing, the damn bastards must be getting reinforcements from the interior of the island by now.' The short man with intense eyes stared us all down one after another, then looked down at the dogs with a doubtful expression and continued gruffly, 'I'm not sure what it is that y'all are supposed to do exactly, I guess just try to help in one way or another, if you can manage. To be honest with you, I feel like I'm sending you fools to the front line to get slaughtered. I've never seen dogs on the battlefield before, but I have my orders from the higher ups to get you out there, so… That will be all men.'

He dismissed us with a salute and we were directed by some daisy new Officer of the exact coordinates on where to meet up with our new forward deployed squads.

Michael looked over at me and said in his Texan accent, 'Here's our chance man, let's go get us some confirmed kills. Let these sunuvabiches know we're here. Ya hear?' I could only chuckle at my friend's enthusiasm as we took the direct paths mapped out for us to Hill D and stayed as quiet as possible as we cautiously worked our way to the front. It was very possible the lines weren't secured and a lone sniper or a couple of guerillas had managed to get missed in the initial sweep and were lying in wait for the chance to strike. I gripped my M1 Garand in both hands as Michael now held on to Cerberus' leash and led the way. The Dobie was as alert as ever and gave us no indication that there were enemies nearby, and after several minutes of hard trekking we came upon two squads of soldiers who were in the midst of placing wounded men on stretchers with blood soaked bandages wrapped around appendages and trying to make hushed radio transmissions.

The Staff Sergeant took notice of us and looked relieved that we were here, at least somebody thought we could be of some use I thought to myself. He motioned over to us and commanded to the man on the radio, 'RJ, RJ... Listen to me God damn it. Order all men in the squads to fall back and regroup here. Now.' Sergeant Schultz then informed us, 'We haven't taken any ground in the last few hours, the Japanese have the zone completely under their control from hidden positions on top of the hill directly in front of us. I tried sending a squad south and see if we could come up around the Jap's field of fire and catch them on their flank, but...' Schultz pointed towards one of his men on a stretcher, the young Marine's bicep was hanging off the bone by a shred of tissue, and as he bit down on a rag to stifle a scream, the medic desperately tightened bandages around the wound, trying to slow the hemorrhaging and hold the muscle back in place on the bone as blood squirted all over him.

I mumbled, 'Ambush?'

Sergeant Schultz answered grimly, 'Yea, got a few of our guys bad. We think there's a machinegun nest on the south side of the hill, and IJA Snipers are hitting everything from the crest. Both squads under my control are tore up and I got about 14 dead or wounded soldiers on my hands. You got any ideas Corporal?'

I looked to Michael and Cerberus, then said, 'Well there aint no reason to worry too much about the machinegun nest if the Snipers are going to pick us off as we try to approach it. Give us whoever can still fight, and we'll take the point and find these Snipers on the hilltop. After we take the high ground, then we can take out the HMG nest with ease.'

The Sergeant liked my confidence as the IJA veterans had sapped it from him and his men with the looming blast of lead from their barrels claiming life after life in the jungle. The losses were quickly mounting and the new plan was to get the wounded and dead back to Schultz's position and then send the rest of us back out with Cerberus, Michael and I on the point and see if we could figure out a way to push forward through the shit. They were pinned down and demoralized, and we were designed to be the force multiplier that could counter these Guerilla Snipers. It was the exact kind of mission we had been trained for from day one at Camp Lejeune, and I was exhilarated to get the opportunity to inflict some damage on the IJA.

However, as the Marines returned from the surrounding forest carrying wounded men and dragging dead bodies back with them, my excitement was dulled by the despair of my brothers and the clear and present dangers that lay ahead. One marine came back with an arm wrapped around a soldier on each side of him as he hobbled forward with a severe leg wound that spouted large quantities of blood. Another soldier staggered backwards with heavy steps as he dragged a limp body through a patch of thickets. A few minutes later, yet another Marine did the same holding a young man under the armpits as he pulled him through the brush into view, with an obvious fatal wound to the head. It was an unsettling scene, but it was how war baptized the warrior; usually in the blood of his own brothers. When the dead were placed on the damp earth and the wounded were being treated by the hectic medic, our Sergeant sent us right back out there into the hell of it all from which his own men had just returned.

I took our Doberman and after pushing through the thick vegetation a few yards, I released Cerberus from his leash so that I wasn't giving away the stealthy dog's position. Michael and I followed about twenty or thirty feet behind the courageous dog as his muscular frame popped in and out of view of the palm leaves and ferns. As the angle of the ground began to rise, transforming into the hillside, the Dobe slowed his progress to a steady rhythm of pausing and listening for signs of enemies and taking a few quick paces to repeat the process. Betal Nut trees and Banana Palms grew in thick groves as the line of Marines stalked through the underbrush with blades slicing away, trying to keep up with the war dog. He eventually froze in position after a few more strides and turned his head to the left with his body rigidly straight. This was the indistinguishable sign the clever dog used to indicate there were enemies close by to the left. Michael halted the squad's advancement with a hand signal and doubled back to explain there were Japanese soldiers about fifty feet to the front of us and an unknown distance to the left. We came up with the proposal to send seven of us back from this current site and then to flank the hidden combatants to the far left, and leave ten soldiers here to lay down suppressive fire and offer a distraction while we came in from the side if shit hit the fan. If we were successful in getting the drop on them, then perhaps we could uproot the IJA Snipers and force them down the hillside into our line of soldiers waiting to finish them off. The group of ten fell back a decent distance and took cover from the sharpshooters behind trunks and thickets of Tangen-Tangen as Cerberus began to lead the rest of us north. It was the only thing we could come up with and if executed properly, we could take out these Hetai who claimed the hill with punishing bullets that had ripped away too many young American lives.

It was nerve racking as we closed in, we couldn't see them, not yet anyways, but Cerberus could and he knew precisely where they were. We traveled about a hundred yards back west and traversed Hill D on a curved trajectory, leaving the bulk of our squad back to take the heat of us as they took shelter from the marksmen. Michael had also advised them not to move forward under any circumstances unless they had an early death wish, but to offer suppressive fire if the IJA hit us first and we had to fall back. We then changed direction and headed east again, this time at a vastly different course so that we could come up on the north side of the hill where hopefully we could pick the hidden sharpshooters apart. They were wreaking havoc on us and it was getting to Sergeant Schultz, I could tell the bodies of his men were piling up on his conscience and he wasn't taking it very well. Cerberus again led our advance on point, this time I was ten to fifteen feet behind him, followed by Michael and the rest of our men in single file as silent as we could manage. Cerberus led us through walls of Coconut trees and through small clearings where beautiful but toxic Angel's Trumpet shrubs dotted the forest floor, and Red Ginger bushes dominated the thickets with fragrant clumps of scarlet blooms attracting shiny Hummingbirds as they zipped in and out of the flowers. After a few hundred yards of navigating the lush foliage of Palms and Staghorn ferns, we got to an area with large deciduous Ifit trees pushing some of the smothering vegetation back and our Doberman halted abruptly and looked down the hill now, the hair on his back bristled as it stood straight, his body nearly shaking with excitement.

I crawled on my elbows up beside the jet black dog and followed his glare down the angle of a couple of degrees to our right. After a few minutes of seeing absolutely nothing, I grew agitated and looked back at Cerberus to see if he was mistaken. The dog didn't break his stance as his nose pointed at the exact same location, his eyes regarded without blinking, his pure intensity demonstrating to me that he was most definitely certain. Cerberus was never unsure, he was a machine, a hunter without equivalent. I asked Michael for his binoculars as he crawled up on the carpet of moldy, dry, leaves, to meet us, and I scanned through the magnified view to approximately where Cerberus stared unrelentingly. Then finally, I found the source of the Doberman's attention after a few more minutes of straining. With the most discreet of motions, I identified a Japanese Sniper covered in a pile of loose leaves as he eyed down his scope, swaying the long Type 38 bolt action rifle from side to side down the hill, looking for American targets to burn. Then as I continued to stare through the binoculars, I eventually made the outline of his spotter just a few feet away tucked into a thorny bush. I analyzed the Sniper team for several more minutes, observing two more Snipers nearby and even found both of their spotters, one of whomes head barely poked out of a mangrove of muddy roots peering through a set of his own binoculars all around the forest. Then the spotter suddenly rotated his binoculars towards our position causing me to duck back behind a tree with my heart racing. My breathing was coming in rushed, erratic huffing, as adrenaline saturated my body. After a short wait, I handed the binoculars to Michael and motioned towards the Japanese Sniper team overlooking the hillside. After a minute or so, he too spotted them and looked at Cerberus with unparalleled appreciation for the majestic dog. In total, I counted six Hetai, which was the slang term we used for Japanese foot soldiers, with three enemy marksman and three spotters armed with Type 100 SMG's or Type 99 Carbines. We signaled to the squad where the Sniper team was located and began setting up for the assault, dragging ourselves inch by inch forward, desperate to not make any disturbance to the natural environment around us that could give us away to the perceptive enemy. I found a nice spot between a tall Ifit and a stunted Lime tree, and placed my M1 Garand on a fallen branch, glaring down the scope at my mortal enemies. We assigned target values and took aim, each at our own marks, making sure all of the

Japanese were covered. Cerberus lay at my side with his head near my arm, I could feel his hot breath on my elbow as he patiently waited, having fulfilled his duty to the most excellent of standards, keeping us from walking into a massacre and then locating the superbly hidden guerilla Snipers.

The seven of us stared down the bores of our rifles at the unsuspecting IJA sharpshooters who were doing the same, and the seconds seemed to turn into hours as we waited for the moment to unleash the barrage. Many of the men who had already watched their countrymen be ripped apart and murdered by this very squad of sharpshooters looked on furiously, ready to seek vengeance on the merciless soldiers. I placed the center of the crosshairs right on top of the sniper's head as it remained nearly enveloped in the pile of leaves where he rested. I adjusted the dial for windage on my M73 scope two clicks left, then slowed my breathing down as I fought against the excitement that rose in my nervous system and spread from my toes to my fingertips. I exhaled slower with each breath, trying to steady my rifle as I inhaled deeply, squeezing the trigger more and more while I exhaled slowly. I could see the leaves rustle with each breath of my enemy, his rifle casting his scope to the west looking for his own target. Then, with my slowest breath yet, I pulled the trigger until I heard the gunpowder detonate with the .30-06 Springfield round exploding through the barrel with a muzzle velocity of 2,800 feet per second. The bullet flew true, smashing into the back of the Japanese Sniper's helmet and shaking his entire body with the aftershocks as the leaves fell from the neat pile that had enshrouded him, revealing the fresh corpse. Like that, the chaos of war rained down on the hidden Japanese soldiers, as more rifle fire let off at the multiple infantrymen remaining. Our machine gunner sprayed indiscriminately as his Browning M1919 GPMG blistered fire down, tearing up the earth in clouds of dust and debris as the 250 rounds were belt fed through the perforated barrel while he guided the powerful monstrosity upon its short tripod.

I pointed my Garand back towards the spotter in the mangroves to realize our shooter designated to him had either missed his mark or placed the shot in a non-vital area. I didn't hesitate to fix my M1 rifle on him as he desperately squirmed away from us through the thicket of tangled roots to disappear back into the rainforest. As he broke free of the roots and began to stand and sprint upright towards a wall of jungle, I laced him in the back with a round right that cut right through the chest as the self-loading gas action piston placed another .30-06 cartridge in the chamber. He had dropped to the ground where he was, but I glanced through the scope past the smoking barrel to see him roll over once, then again back to his stomach on all fours. I could see a gaping exit wound in the front of his chest that would no doubt prove fatal as it had decimated his rib cage and blew out the majority of his right lung through the vivid red hole that continued to pour out a mixture of blood, bits of organs, and even shards of splintered bone. The Japanese soldier refused to give up though, and crawled towards the foliage, but remorselessly, mechanically, I squeezed off another round into the wounded man. This time, after the earsplitting crack of thunder, he didn't move again.

Chapter 2

Throughout our first day on the Island, our commanding Officers kept us busy in the turmoil and havoc of all-out battle between the enraged IJA enemy and our forceful invasion. On our next mission we were assigned to escort a Platoon of Marines between two access roads through an incredibly dense section of forest. Cerberus led us swiftly through practically impenetrable jungle as the entire Platoon followed in our path, fortunately without incident as the battle was all around us. In many other zones, the Japanese Army was refusing to fall back any further and valiant stands were made against the beachheads to try and thwart our momentum. Their eyes in the jungle and dangerous fortifications made advancing at any steady pace a perilous endeavor. Many of these stands were repelling our attacks from concealed locations near Gaan Point or Maanot Ridge, Snipers hid in the folds of cliffs, Riflemen rolled grenades down inclines, and machinegun nests sprayed enfilading fire from the crest of rocky precipices, turning the bluffs into nightmarish castle towers. The IJA's advanced scouts were camouflaged with the rainforest and directing demoralizing mortar fire towards our newly arriving forces when proficiently directed. Any of our major forces being assembled that could be pinpointed by their scouts were being hailed with 81mm combustible HE rounds from their Type 99 Mortars to a deadly degree, impaling our troops with shrapnel and leaving our vehicles as warped wreckage. It didn't help matters that massive IJA Type 96 Howitzers positioned far from the front lines were obliterating our soldiers, artillery, and armor in hellish explosions, the 22 foot long 9,000 pound guns were lobbing 15 cm artillery rounds tenaciously. These defensive maneuvers and counter attacks put immense pressure on the front lines to push on towards the enemies' big guns further inland and on the higher ground, which only served to make the Japanese ambushes that much more effective as we rushed onward. Numerous squads were caught off guard and mowed down by the heavy machinegun fire or point blank sniping of the concealed Imperial Army. The gains were slow and bloody, if there were gains at all, and forging ahead without counterattacks was all but impossible, that is unless a U.S. Marine War Dog unit was attached to the advance.

Not long after our first contact with the enemy, First Lieutenant Dunham had bragged of the success our Scouting Unit provided to his squads over the wire communications to our superiors and after our latest escort assignment, we were immediately reattached to a Platoon half a mile south of us that had run into resistance. Cerberus, Michael, and I began our journey towards our new directive. From the way it sounded, the Platoon whose objective was taking a trail and securing a river valley in their zone had come into complications with an unknown amount of adversaries manning some kind of fortifications in the wetlands. Our briefing was hazy at best, and I figured we could gather much more information when we arrived. As we marched peering into the dark, light absorbing crevices of undergrowth all around us, I looked at Cerberus while Michael gripped his leash, the canine's muscular back legs propelled him forward effortlessly pulling his handler with his long strides. After a while, we stopped for a quick break as Michael poured some water from his dull green canteen into the cupped palm of his hand for the awaiting, thirsty, dog as he joyfully wagged his nubby tail and lapped the water up. I took a sip of the cool, crisp, water from my own canteen and regarded the content disposition displayed on the Doberman's long face, his pronounced, clean, white teeth shined with his jowls pulled back into a distinctive smile. Michael too took notice of the energetic and content dog and said to me in his southern drawl, 'Damn, it's almost like this Doberman was made for this shit, huh.'

I laughed and answered, 'There ain't many who are cut out for war, but I will say this. That Doberman seems to enjoy it, the crazy pup.' Cerberus' ears perked up as if he knew we were talking about him, and as playful as he was, his work drive hungered to get a move on as his restless demeanor twitched down every carved muscle of the intimidating canine.

Michael continued, 'It's like he don't even tire none, not even in this heat. He's meaner than a wet panther I tell ya. Look at 'em, he's rearing to go for more. Would you believe dat?'

'There hasn't been a day to go by yet where this boy hasn't impressed me, I guess he's just taking it up a level now that we're in the real thing. And thank God for that.' I replied.

Lance Corporal Michael nodded and as we got ready to move out, he said over his shoulder, 'Hey man, I just wanted to say, that was a good tactical advance back there on them Snipers. Really, you two done a good job gettin us in position to kill them Japs. Fine shootin too man. Just wanted to say that.'

Realizing Michael Blanchet wasn't one to pay compliments often, I nodded towards Cerberus and said, 'Thanks man, I just followed our war dog's nose and made the decisions we were trained to do, and it worked out for the best.' I adjusted my stuffy helmet and readied my rifle as we walked through the overhanging vines and greenery.

Michael looked back over his shoulder while Cerberus moved us forward and returned, 'Well if the creek don't rise none, then how the hell are we gunna get into the real fun with these boys?' Again I laughed, me and Michael may not have always gotten along during our intensive training with Cerberus at Camp Lejeune, but he was a good man, and I was glad he was watching over us with his Thompson, knowing he'd lay down his life for us just like we would do the same for him. We focused back to the cold reality that lay at our feet, and moved quickly through the bush, jumping into a scorched crater and climbing over a fallen tree whose leaves were singed clean off, while our Doberman cleared the wide trunk with a single bound like it wasn't even there.

After several more minutes of navigating to the checkpoint, we eventually came upon a group of fourteen men and a dog all crouched low against another fallen tree. Most of them looked spooked out of their minds, so we eased up until the Doberman and his handlers noticed us in order to get their attention. When they seen us, I could see many of their faces were pale as a ghost, and they gestured for us to get over to them and stay low. When we reached them, the Officer found his way over to us under the wet, termite infested, rotted log in a military crawl. He introduced himself, 'Hello men, I'm Chief Warrant Officer McDermont, I'm glad you're here. I heard you were able to locate and neutralize a Sniper team to our north that was giving our men trouble.' We confirmed his question as he continued in a frantic manner, 'That's great news, good to hear. I have my hands full and my Platoon has been getting hammered from all sorts a shit. We just don't have a clue how they're tearing us apart, but I'm guessing they got some machine gunners and Snipers working in teams, perhaps a command post or something as well. They just keep outflanking us...' The Officer's words were interrupted as a rifle blast roared through the air close by with echoes reverberating off the trees. A few of the men jumped from the sound, Officer McDermont hesitated, staring into nothingness momentarily before he went on, 'They keep outflanking us quicker than we can move in, it doesn't make any God damn sense. I'd like your advanced recon unit to see if you can lead a patrol an gather some intel of what exactly are we facing over here in this river basin.'

I voiced to McDermont, 'Well sir, Cerberus here is already indicating enemy troops all around us in the bush, not far either, so this is definitely a major point of resistance. Those Hetai guerillas are still out there and waiting.' The stone gargoyle of a dog stood at attention with the group of men, his piercing eyes darting around the jungle as his snout lifted an inhaled the multitude of odors floating in the humid air, tracking the concealed soldiers in ways they had never predicted.

The Chief Warrant Officer looked at Cerberus with pleading eyes as he warned us, 'Half my Platoon got scattered about 50 yards to the south by machine gunners, we got a lot of wounded, and more than likely even more are dead. I got over a quarter of my men trying to get to the survivors, so watch for friendly fire. I can give you ten men and our Messenger Dog Unit to assist your reconnaissance, and I can send more your way when the rest of my guys return. I'll keep one of the handlers with me and you can communicate to us through their dog, Arno. It's a God damn mess out there, so be careful.'

Michael and I decided to take our newly formed squad to the north east away from the chaos just south of us, better to avoid the chance of friendly fire in either direction if we could. I also figured the Japanese were ruthless enough to wait it out with the survivors, keeping an eye on them and if any help arrived, then they too would be picked off as the rescuers responded to their wounded brethren in need. The ten regular Marine Privates, one dog handler, and his sleek messenger Doberman filed in line behind us as we moved out. They were covered in mud and scrapes, shaken up by the latest ambush, but they were willing and able to fight on, and that was all that mattered. During a pause for a quick meeting, I debriefed one of the men in almost inaudible whispers to get a better feel for what was out there. The Private First Class, Antoine said with wide eyes, 'The Platoon had been making it through the swampy shit with ease, no hiccups.' He stopped and pointed out to the east in the tall Russel River grass and Staghorn ferns, where we could periodically hear the screams of our injured men somewhere out there as they called for help, laying in puddles covered by the shrubs and ferns while bleeding away. If we were going to be able to get to any of them before they bled to death, then it was imperative that we worked fast. Private Antoine continued, almost angrily, 'Well then about fifty yards that way, all hell broke loose. We couldn't get a read on em, it was like they were popping up from nowhere all around us, automatic fire from all sides.' I thanked the Private for sharing his experience, and proceeded on with the push.

Cerberus led us out of the marsh and onto a barely noticeable trail that blended into the overgrowth, we followed it with our boots landing agonizingly softly on the dry, crunchy, decaying leaves with each step. The Doberman's sharp ears rotated like radar dishes picking up the faintest sounds as he forged ahead. The squad crouched and slowed as the War Dog picked up the scent of a nearby enclave, signaling to it by freezing in place and pointing his head straight ahead, towards a profusion of tropical shrubs. As we lowered all the way to the ground and dragged ourselves to the edge of the shrubbery, we poked our heads through a thicket of thorny branches and realized the astonishing Doberman had brought us right on top of a provisional fortress filled with Japanese soldiers.

Michael and I stayed low in the brush as we counted out the clearly visible soldiers, and not wanting to make a fatal mistake, took our time scanning the tree lines and dense bushes all around the compound. It wasn't much of a fortress, but when correctly utilized by the experienced and hardened Japanese Army, it was a real killing field. We made out two fresh, shallow trenches that stretched away a hundred yards in each direction from a central point of bamboo shacks that were erected behind the sturdy, cylindrical, bunker of a stone pillbox filled with soldiers manning two heavy machineguns. The bivouacked, bamboo structures were primitive with thatched roofs of palm fronds and offered shelter for supplies and gear, with boxes of ammunition and rations of food clearly visible through the unfinished walls. To the rear of the pillbox and small huts was a rickety bridge that hung over the brown water of the tributary that ran along the backside of the Japanese defenses. The trenches were hastily dug with churned soil evident the entire length of them, and they were certainly using the sunken channels to quickly and safely run troops to intercept our forces stuck in the wetland's thick brush and knee deep swamp, with the swampy foreground acting as an entrapping kill zone the closer you made it to the compound. The trenches themselves were running at an obtuse angle from the pillbox, using the river basin as a natural funnel towards their crafty setup of demise for any who wondered in-between the intricate crossfire. What caught my attention more than the shallow trench system was the deadly spider holes that dotted behind and in front of it about every twenty yards. Each nearly unseen hole was covered in sticks and branches with a Japanese soldier squatting inside, peering through the veil of mothernature and ready to spring out and unload their dependable Type 99 light machineguns into any unsuspecting Marine that dare come their way. These defenses allowed the Japanese to provide cover fire for one another and would make for an un-survivable disaster for any who fell victim to the widespread and sophisticated ambush.

Higher on the river banks just out of the basin, our vantage point allowed us to examine and scour every square foot of the fortifications, as Michael jotted down on a notepad an illustration to scale as best he could, of exactly what we saw from his binoculars. I trained my rifle scope from spider hole to spider hole, deciphering the oddities only a trained eye for recon could make. My eyes honed in on the against the grain brush cover from my elevated perspective that a man walking on the flats would be completely unable to spot before it was too late. Translated to paper, it made for an impressive, obscured, fortress of barricades, posts, and hidden foxholes that interweaved perfectly into the natural surroundings, and as hard as it would be; we would have to find a way to infiltrate it all. We even located a pair of Snipers on the tree line behind the bamboo shacks near the cloudy river. During this entire time that we put our advance recon skills to the test, there was the occasional spout of gunshots to the south of us as the majority of our platoon was still mired in combat, stuck in the bloody quagmire of Japanese crosshairs and itchy trigger fingers.

After a thorough examination of every troop we were up against, it appeared there were nineteen concealed spider holes, twenty four soldiers in the trenches, two snipers on the riverbank, and a fortified pill box of several men operating a pair of Model 1 HMGs. The two 7.7 mm heavy machineguns pointed out of their loopholes at overlapping angles, with the HMG's controlling the battlefield with brutal firepower. We were up against an entire Imperial Army Platoon dug in and ready to end any Marines' life that went against them. Michael and I conferred with the Messenger, Private Jefferson about our ever evolving strategy to dissect the Japanese defenses. The best move we could think of was to try and surprise attack the compound, though this would prove almost impossible since the alert enemy already knew we were in the area and were prepared to fire at anything that moved. We figured the only route to take was the one they wouldn't be expecting, because coming at their defensive positions from the front was an obvious recipe for total annihilation. Jefferson agreed with our tactics and scribbled down an encoded message of our plan of action as well as the intel gathered, that he then placed within Arno's specialized collar. With a pat on the back from Jefferson, Arno instantly disappeared into the foliage to meet his other handler so that he could interpret the coded message to our Commanding Officer. I began to line up some of our marksmen onto the overlooking riverbank to maintain surveillance for target acquisition as we waited.

Fifteen minutes later, the faithful Doberman reemerged from the bushes in a stealthy trot, Cerberus was already waiting, happy to welcome the other Military dog. Arno weaved out the trees and through the troops straight towards Private Jefferson without a second thought. He bent to one knee and greeted the panting dog by petting his ears while he withdrew the new message from the other handler. Lance Corporal Jefferson deciphered it, telling us that Chief Warrant Officer McDermont had good news, he approved of our plan of attack, and better yet most of his Marines had returned. There were details that had to be worked out, so once again Arno was eagerly sent back into the treacherous jungle, dodging overhead blast of automatic fire, this time to return the pillbox coordinates within the coded communications. We waited on the river bank in the bush, tense and nervous all while rapid volleys sounded in the near distance across the marsh. When Arno returned from his journey of sprinting through the surrounding combat in the swamps, Officer McDermont's message declared bad news this time, stating that the communications had been down for the last hour and he had been unable to raise contact with any of our mortar teams or artillery to try and knockout the pillbox. Still, with time a crucial factor due to the wounded men we couldn't reach, the Officer agreed to our request to commence without artillery support, and issued an order for Cerberus, Michael and I to come back to them and lead the platoon safely back to our current location to reinforce our location with a few more sharpshooters before we attempted the daring raid.

We left the group of eleven soldiers and winded messenger dog at the observation position and drove back through the wilderness on the outskirts of the swamp, essentially the way we had first come. Cerberus was as alert as ever, and zig zagged us around several areas that were now crawling with Japanese infantry. The Doberman signaled more than once to a few areas where enemies were hiding in the trenches as we crept past them, not wanting to engage them and give up the element of surprise just yet. We found twenty eight men now at the fallen tree with Officer McDermont. He looked at the three of us with gratitude and new hope as we hurriedly joined up with the Platoon and began guiding them through the tropical marshland's mangroves, an endless tangle of stilt roots formed by the Nipa Palms and Loop-root shrubs as we sloshed through the warm water. The river basin was developing a mounting intensity as the Japanese infantry became agitated with the stall in action. The IJA were uncomfortable, and grew irritated as to where the Platoon had gone, their paranoia rising as they searched the mangrove swamp for Marines to slaughter, but they simply couldn't find any. They expected another frontal assault by blind troops, but instead Cerberus steered us around their traps, avoiding the ambushes one after another. The dog was hypervigilant, his phenomenal senses tuned in a manner that put us a step ahead of our fanatical enemy. Cerberus' solid, lengthy, frame yanked me by the leash as he inhaled the air like it was pungent perfume radiating off a beautiful woman, and snapping his head to the side to better listen to the faint breaths of foes or the slightest snap of a twig hundreds of feet away. He changed course several times as the black and rust canine somehow managed to get all thirty of our Marines back to the riverbank where our squad anxiously awaited.

The Japanese Army was incensed, they knew we were in the river basin with them, they just didn't know where. They couldn't find us, and it was entirely due to the unreal scout dog that kept us all alive, even though we were literal steps from walking into a slaughter if we so much as veered a short distance from the path that he shepherd. We were his flock and the Imperial Japanese Army were the ravenous wolves that sought our lives, paid for in bullets and blood. With our scouting unit altering everything, it would be interesting to see if we could now become the hunters in this new form of evolving combat. We were men being led by a beast in only the way an animal can lead, and it was giving us unprecedented advantages on the ugly battlefield. When we arrived at the site, we formulated the last several calculations and communicated to every Marine what their role was as we tensed up for the raid. Because of my superior marksmanship, Officer McDermont wanted me to stay here on the sniper location, and added a few more rifles to give us eight sharpshooters, and two spotters. I hated to relinquish my handling duty of the dog I had become so accustomed to, even if it was temporary, but I understood my abilities would best be suited on the overlooking riverbank where I could put my Garand to good use.

The other thirty men would go south east, escorted by Cerberus and Michael along the slow flowing, muddy river. It was our collective decision that in order to save any of the wounded men that could still be alive out there in the swamp, we had to first neutralize this compound and all the soldiers patrolling the grounds. We hoped it would be possible to sneak a force of men in from behind and avoid the deadly entrapments and buzz saw of heavy machinegun fire that they utilized. We would wait for our forces led by Cerberus to sneak as close as possible and then our marksman would hit them as hard as we could with sniper fire to distract the Japanese as we rushed Marines at them from their unguarded weak points. It was beyond dangerous, but with lives weighing in the balance out there in the marsh, I don't think any of us thought there was a choice.

I gave Cerberus a rough head patting and told Michael, 'Good luck man, wait for my signal and give them hell.' As the men departed for their excursion into the river, I crawled to the center of our line of sharpshooters, knowing we had one chance at this, and we had to make it count. The spotters and snipers were communicating about atmospheric conditions, wind and distances, but I was checking on the Sniper team on the river bank behind the huts. I found out who was taking out the one on the left, and a young man assured me he had him. I blurted harshly, 'Don't tell me you do, show me. We can't miss these shots and lose those Snipers in all the mayhem, we got to take them out first, or they will be taking us out.' I knew I was being hard on the kid, but the last time we had almost let a Sniper slip away and once your position is given away it could have cost us dearly, especially when your men start getting counter sniped by the hidden marksmen.

I went through the squad making sure everyone was set and ready before I crawled up into position, dragging myself forward an inch, then slowing to a centimeter by centimeter crawl, parting a shrub a single round, waxy, leaf at a time with my barrel as I concentrated my aim on the furthest marksman enshrouded in the tall yellow grass beside the river. I stayed masked in the shrubs as I turned the knob four clicks right for windage, then the elevation adjustment one slow *click, click, click,* at a time, trying to calculate the distance and trajectory just right. The further the mark and greater the distance, all the more I needed to dial in so that the bullet strike would be that much closer to perfection, ensuring the kill of a dangerous nemesis. Satisfied, I put the crosshairs right on my adversary's dome. One of the spotters made visual of our troops moving coyly up the river, immersed to their waist in the calm, warm waters. They were brave men, fighting the current quite literally, and my hands became sweaty as I realized our strikes from this team would decide the life and death outcome for many of our Marines about to storm the fortifications. They got closer and closer to the bamboo huts pressed up against the river, and a perfect silence fell over my squad as I pinpointed an exact spot on my target hundreds of yards away. One of our spotters finally said in a shaky whisper, 'They're in position.'

I replied, 'On my mark.' I held my breath, the breeze brushed by my face as I stared at the cross of my M73 scope until it branded itself into the Imperial Sniper a thousand feet from me, and just squeezed the kill switch. The M1 Garand jolted against my shoulder, followed by simultaneous blast from the line of rifles on my sides, lacing the unsuspecting troops before they knew what hit them. From the scope optic I witnessed the hidden marksman's face morph into an inhuman atrocity of gore, concaving his nose and eye sockets to the back of his skull with a violent expansion of kinetic energy transferred by the .30-06 round as the chunk of metal burst out the back of his skull, rearranging his face into space that his brain matter once occupied. Judging by the low shot trajectory, I must have miscalculated the distance, but it was still an enemy down and I swiveled my instrument of war right on to the next ill-fated opponent. Our first shots served to disembowel the opposition's most lethal and prepared infantry, and we rapidly moved our rifles to new targets while the enemy was still in shock as the bitter odor of gun powder circulated around us in the bushes.

At the same time our Marines rushed out of the river upon the compound as all the attention was pulled to the north in an attempt to identify the source of the shots. They sloshed up the small incline and the thirty soldiers ran between the huts and then right on top of the trench system and circular stone pillbox as they let their machine guns do the talking. One of the Marines tossed a bouncing Pineapple Grenade into the open loophole from which a brand new Type 1 heavy machinegun aimed out of, away from the river where the Platoon approached from. Not to be outdone, yet another heroic soldier sprinted around the pillbox and dropped his own MK2 Pineapple grenade into the opening just feet from the giant barrel of one of the machineguns as he ducked under it and ran. There were burst of rapid shots as our boys got the jump on the dazed infantry, spraying from their M3 Grease guns and M1 Thompson trenchsweepers as they poured .45 ACP rounds by the thirty round clips into the dugouts of men. ***Boom***!... ***Booom***!!... One thunderous explosion followed in succession by another rocked the fortified pillbox as thick, black, smoke drifted from the loopholes where the now mangled Model 1 heavy machineguns protruded from, rendered useless to the ongoing battle.

I fixed my M1 Garand lower, hundreds of feet from my first shot and placed it right on top of one of the nearest spider holes to the advancing platoon. I stabilized my aim and waited, delaying my agonizing desire to empty the chamber right then and there. With my open eye squinting hard through the scope, I zeroed in on my prey, trying to get just a glimpse. Then as I centered it over the delicately construed branches and leaves intertwined with strands of grass, the spider hole shattered open with twigs and leaves flying away as an IJA soldier popped out leveling his Type 100 submachine gun Shiki Kikan-Tanju at our incoming Marines. In the split second it took him to shoot at our exposed men, it was already too late as I let off a Springfield round that penetrated through the back of his neck, jerking his head left and severing the spinal column, ending the Hetai's life instantly. His head flopped sideways as his body dropped limply back into the hollow pit with a thud, the spider hole now serving as his shallow grave. Our men moved deeper into the dregs taking out more soldiers as they did so with their SMG's blazing the paths. I swung my Garand to the side and placed a quick shot into a crouched foot soldier as he hurried up the muddy trench to offer support to his surprised comrades. The shot sank square into his chest causing him to fall flat on his face as the Garand reloaded another cartridge into the chamber for me to place into its next victim.

Our men were making headway through the compound as the Japanese began to reorganize their defensive positions all while the multitude of their backline was absorbing our bullets in the frenzy. I continued to rain down shots on the enemy, skimming a sprinting soldier with a round, then finding his center with the next dropping his wounded body to the earth where he thrashed about in agony, mixing the mud with crimson gore that leaked from his abdomen. The Imperial army was still fighting courageously as a soldier exploded from another spider hole and shot up two of our men with his Type 100 submachine gun cutting up the Marines with 8mm Nambu ammo flying from the perforated chrome barrel as he caught them by surprise. I aimed down my scope on the assailant but before I could shoot, one of our men had torn him apart with his M1918 BAR, shredding the soldier to pieces with the majority of the twenty round box. I quickly trained my rifle back towards the northern trench as our soldiers continued to overrun it. I delivered another round with a rocketing reminder of our marksmanship from the higher riverbank, sending fearsome thunderbolts of death down with precision upon the battleground.

The Japanese were uprooted from their northern trench and those that tried to run for the southern trench were mowed down by the devil's piano, automatic fire leaving nothing untouched. After another minute of brutal exchanges, we had completely taken the northern trench and now turned our full attention to the southern sector. The surviving Japanese soldiers ducked down in the southern trench, with seasoned veterans unloading their bolt action Arisaka Type 38 rifles with great accuracy, plunging 6.5 x 50 mm rounds into the hearts and heads of any soldier standing too high in the opposite trench system. Others pulled the pins and tossed their Type 91 and Type 10 grenades across the diverging grounds, littering the swampy fields in explosions of shrapnel as our soldiers dove for cover, with some too late to escape the fragmentation blasts of scorching shrapnel. I found Cerberus and Michael at the forefront of the action, near where the trenches conjoined at the pillbox bunker. They ducked down behind the muddy walls of the trench, where occasionally Michael would let off a couple shots of suppressive fire. That's when I noticed a squad of Imperial foot soldiers readying to charge the closest part of the north trench where my Scouting unit comrades held. I swung the barrel and started taking aim as the Japanese sprang from their southern trench and implemented a banzai attack with their bayonetted rifles firing and their screams audibly brash. I fired my first shot, a jarring blast from the M1 Garand as it pierced the forward most fighter and collapsed him to the marshy grass. I flicked the barrel a quarter inch to the side and focused the cross on the next man, but the squad of IJA hadn't even flinched and continued their mad dash to assault the opposite trench.

I could see Cerberus dropping lower as Michael pushed the canine down as far out of harm's way as he could while separately spraying the aggressors with the Thompson, dropping two in a row with a powerful SMG burst of .45 ACP. I directed my Garand at yet another of the fanatical soldiers on the run and led him the slightest bit before releasing the cartridge in a detonation of gunpowder as the velocity of the round knocked the infantryman over sideways into a final barrel roll in the slippery muck. My Garand sounded off its telltale *ping* that indicated its eight round clip was spent, so I hurriedly yanked out the empty clip and jammed in a full en bloc in the top-loading receiver as I could only watch the attack unfold. Thankfully, several of Michael's nearby comrades took up the challenge with him and laid down devastating strafing from their Browning Automatic Rifles as streams of .30-06 lead projectiles slammed into the line of Japanese, the LMGs chopping them down on the run. Still a few of the Japanese soldiers from the original fifteen made the length of the disastrous crossing and now stood over the trench lighting up our men with their Type 99 Light Machineguns, damning three consecutive men with well-placed 7.7 x 58 mm Arisaka rounds, splattering blood everywhere, including on my nearby Marine Dog Scouting unit. Michael was able to drop the first two crazed Japanese soldiers to their knees with a flash of gunshots from his Trench Sweeper until the clip ran dry, with only empty clicks coming from the weapon.

Crouching down with my Doberman, the two were exposed to the wrath of the last bloodthirsty soldier standing over him with his machinegun swinging towards their heads. Suddenly the Hetai dropped his weapon as it swung like a pendulum while it stayed slung around his shoulder by its strap, and clutched at his heart. My shot had sliced clean through the man's side, cutting through his heart and exiting out of his chest in a disturbing mess. The young Japanese man, barely twenty years of age, fell into the trench at Michael's feet, gasping for air in his last throws of a life cut short by war.

We continued hailing down sniper rounds off the embankment, picking off the enemy with constant rifle fire from undisclosed sites in the shrubs and bushes. Meanwhile our Platoon was utilizing the cover fire and making strong advances as they pushed from the bunker down the southern trench with grenades, carbines, and light machine guns constantly clearing out the spider holes and trench dwellers. We ate through their defenses with an absurd amount of bullets and explosions that their infantry just couldn't handle, as they continuously fell back or fell down. It was an encouraging change as we swept through the entire compound with growing momentum, a few of the last remaining Japanese even ran towards the final stages of the raid. Most of the others fought to the bitter end, not willing to dishonor their Emperor or become prisoners of war. With the last sounds of gun fire subsiding, our Marines had claimed the compound as the last of the IJA slipped back into the jungle. We had taken down a major encampment with solid defenses, and now the task of rounding up our wounded out in the swamp became our next mission.

Our soldiers secured the compound up to the river with post and guards as a few Snipers remained in position offering observation while the rest of the troops started sweeping the swampy brush for our injured and fallen brothers. Cerberus did a hell of a job as he rapidly found some of our wounded, pulling me straight towards those who were still hanging on, time and again. Some of the bodies we found were cold, blue, and deceased as we were simply too late, but those who were alive were receiving immediate medical attention from our medics as we plotted out ways to get them to the medical tents to the west where they could be better taken care of and stabilized. Overall the battle had saved about as many lives as it had cost, with the Platoon's numbers down to thirty two live soldiers, though about a third of them were wounded and needed serious medical attention from the doctors. Still it was a hell of an early victory against a foe who wasn't giving an inch without claiming American blood, so it was good to blow it wide open for once, running through the Japanese defenses and showing our resolve. McDermont congratulated Michael and I and told us his Platoon would await reinforcements here and become an auxiliary force for the newly arriving Platoons.

We began exploring the bivouacked encampment of bamboo structures behind all the bunker and trench defenses while we waited, turning up weapons and ammunition along with stockpiles of rice. Apparently one of the men located a mineshaft type hidden entrance under a table in one of the huts, and Cerberus, Michael and I were assigned to the cave to see if it was occupied with any IJA. Our stunning Doberman brought us through the front entrance and we slid the table to the side as the dog smelled into the manmade cavern. The dog gave no suggestion of anyone inside, so I left the two of them there and slipped down into the barely shoulder wide opening with my Colt 1911 handgun drawn. Inside the cool fissure, I found empty bunks and a small torch on the wall throwing flickering shadows throughout the hollow room, and other than a light machinegun with the bayonet hilt attached under the barrel and some dry blankets, there was nobody in the cave so I made my way up the ladder back into the humid jungle air. I handed the Type 99 light machinegun to Michael and said, 'All clear. Cerberus was right, empty but for some cots and spider webs. Definitely not one of the weapon caches we're looking for.'

Michael complained, 'I don't like those little cave thing-a-majigs and shit, be gettin too damn claustrophobic to be going in too many ah those.'

I reiterated, 'Well it's part of the job, and you got the next one we come across.'

We both let out some boisterous laughter with Michael saying, 'Yea, well in that case I'm not going down there without dropping some MK2 Pineapples in first.' He chuckled again and walked out the back door of the hut holding the Japanese weapon, and before I could respond he took a few steps to the right and stepped on a switch. A bent bamboo pole was released from the concealing leaves and its potential energy flung a heavy end full of honed punji stakes upwards, smashing into Michael's face as he stood over the booby-trap. I looked out through the hut's open walls in horror to see the sharpened bamboo stakes driven inches deep into my friend's face and throat, as he was caught in his stance, screaming in agony as the trap's spikes remained lodged in his face. Cerberus burst through the back door to his handler, agitated and unable to do anything. I ran right behind him up to Michael as his hands grasped at the sickening and simplistic bamboo instrument. I grimaced as I studied the lethal aftermath while Michael gasped for air only to choke on his own blood, I couldn't decide what to do, whether to try and pull it off of him or try to keep him from struggling and moving any more. Cerberus looked from Michael to me as I yelled at the top of my lungs, 'Medic!! I need a God damn medic over here now!' Michael's face was swathed in blood, it gushed from under his eyes where the top two punji stakes had entered his face, and it squirted almost mercifully from where the bottom two stakes gouged into his throat. I again desperately beseeched, 'We need a fucking medic! Medic, stat!' The design was rudimentary, its intentions insidious, and the results were catastrophic. In the horror of it all, I could only watch in anguish as my friend's suffering slowly ceased in the torturous predicament, until his last breath seemed to have transpired.

Chapter 3

I was exhausted, mentally and physically fatigued through the first day of combat with the furious IJA. The sun was setting on the horizon, shining brilliant rays of light that sliced through the crevices of the trees in shifting patterns that swayed in the breeze. Not even a full day on Guam and I had already lost one of my best friends, and his death had been hard to take under the circumstances. The shock of combat and Michael's passing had coalesced into something of a living nightmare inside my mind, as the horrific event replayed with the honed punji stakes impaling themselves into my friend's face over and over in my head. Cerberus and I had watched in utter disbelief as the medic and his assistant had pulled the bamboo stakes out of his face and gently laid him to the ground where they attempted to resuscitate the fallen Marine for the next fifteen minutes. It was of no use though, they gave up to tend to the other wounded soldiers still breathing, and I helped to move his bloody corpse to the makeshift arrangements for the dead and wounded as they waited on stretcher bearers and reinforcements to arrive before shipping them back west to the main force. It was hard on Cerberus as well, he just didn't seem to understand why his second handler wouldn't acknowledge him when he flipped his hand encrusted in dried blood on top of his nose as he nuzzled the dead soldier. He even placed his large paw onto Michael's chest in an attempt to awake his deceased master as the cadaver laid lifeless on the ground. I realized that all the training together, the talks in the galleys of the naval ships across the pacific, the last letters to our families back home that we held for one another in case of such instances; they were all only memories now. I embraced the somber dog, rubbing the thick fur on his neck before retrieving my own letter that I had wrote from Michael's coat. I placed it in the same pocket that I stored his letter to his wife and parents, and thought of how I would go about contacting them and delivering his final written words. That is if I made it off this God forsaken extinct volcanic island at all. I looked over Michael's corpse one last time, it was difficult to take in with his mutilated face barely recognizable, but Cerberus and I said our goodbyes respectfully in the dimming light and reported back to duty.

Like that, our scouting unit was down to just Cerberus and myself, and it was up to us to continue the fight where our fallen brothers had left off. I wanted to sleep more than ever before, but as the sun descended and sent the darkness crawling over the landscape, my new Gunner Sergeant had informed me that Cerberus was needed near a front line post a quarter mile south. Before departing the area, I walked over to the booby-trap where the blood had collected, running down the bamboo poles where it had been dispersed on the ground by Michael's kicking feet. I picked up the Japanese LMG from the ground that Michael had been carrying, shouldered it and then studied the layout of the wicked trap, looking for any detail that could give it away in the future. After one last look at the scene where I watched my friend die brutally, I was traveling in solitude with only my dog through the murky forest to meet with the next company. Though the jungle was even more obscuring and confusing at night, my Doberman Pinscher was completely unaffected by this enormous change, as his eye's glowed eerily white and his dark body blended seamlessly with the shadows. His superior night vision combined with his already unparalleled abilities to hear and smell were reliable enough to depend on with your life, even in the darkest of nights. He heard every rat that scurried in the grass below, he smelled every bird perched in the canopy above, and Cerberus sure as hell could pinpoint any one of these IJA soldiers hiding all around us. I didn't enjoy marching in the late hours, I felt clumsy in the pitch black under the heavy rainforest canopy, and though I pushed loudly through the bushes at times or stumbled awkwardly over roots and dips in the ground, my dog prevented these follies from ending us as he guided me safely to our destination.

The closer we came to the coordinates of our new company, they more often we heard the random buzz of machine guns cut through the quietness of the woodland. Eventually we neared the company's encampment, I looked down at Cerberus as we entered a clearing and the moonlight was finally able to reach us for the first time since we began our journey. The moon's soft lunar light splashed on the Doberman's rugged physique, shining off his glossy coat from his docked tail all the way up to his horned ears. It was apparent that this war dog was as much in his element nocturnally as he was in the midafternoon glare of day, nothing would stop the Doberman from persisting on. We radioed the company from a hundred feet away, wary from being mistaken for the enemy by the rattled guards in the night conditions. Minutes later they welcomed us in and we entered the forward outpost which wasn't much for quarters at all. There were a few tents and about two hundred Marines of F Company dug into personal foxholes and small dirt bunkers as nearly every one of them seemed to be wide awake and on edge. They surrounded Cerberus and me with smiles and handshakes as we represented a strange curiosity on the frontlines, but one that fascinated and impressed many of the men. After fifty handshakes and about a hundred Marines asking to pet the Doberman Pinscher or inquiring an endless list of questions about the dog and how we worked together, a Sergeant finally found me in the crowd. He told the men to back off and helped us find our way to the biggest bunker. There I met with the Commanding Officer in the middle of the hurriedly formed outpost. The chunky, older man approached me with a salute, then a firm handshake and introduced himself, 'Greetings Corporal, I'm Major Davis of the 22nd Marines. Welcome to my Rifle Company, I assume you're part of the War Dog Platoon that our Marines are praising so much of late, you've built up quite a reputation in just a single day.'

I answered gravely, 'Not without great sacrifice, Sir. We lost the other handler of Cerberus here, not too long ago.'

Major Davis looked at Cerberus who sat loyally by my side and paused before looking back to me, 'I'm sorry to hear that son, it's been a rough day for most of our Division. These Japs don't want to give up this island without a fight. Speaking of which, the IJA have been organizing hit and run squads against us ever since dusk, and we haven't landed a shot yet. Close to two thousand shots fired and all we've managed to hit is a fucking Water Buffalo! They killed a few of my guys on the southern side of our east perimeter just before dark, then ten minutes later they pop outta the jungle and hit us on the north side and retreated before we could so much as aim our rifles. And it's been getting worse, seems like each attack emboldens them further, these Japs won't let up. Been infiltrating our eastern perimeter from the jungle since dark, and the shittiest thing of it all is we can't find them, not even a hint. My boys have been dumping an ammo depot into the damn trees for nothing, and as you can imagine, it's hard for my men to sleep.'

I replied, 'I see, so where do you want us, Sir?'

'Well I've asked for some sentry dogs to help out with the situation, but I was told their ETA would be a couple hours. That's why you're here, you were the closest Military Dog Unit in the area, and I would like for you to take a squad and maintain security on our eastern perimeter until the sentry dogs can arrive to relieve you.' Davis said.

I answered, 'No problem, Cerberus and I can handle that.'

The Major responded, 'I know it's a lot to ask this late, and I also know you're normally an advance scout recon unit, so it means a helluva lot to this company son. Really, we haven't been able to counter these bastards in the night, and they know it. I hope you have better luck.' He showed me to the squad that would be under me and we made our way to the eastern perimeter to try and instill some order for the anxious Company. Honestly I was quite aggravated with the mission, I was irritable as hell and wanted some sleep in the worst way, and this type of detail was way below what we were trained to do. Cerberus and I were special advance reconnaissance, a search and destroy unit, but if it saved any more of our troops' lives, then it was still an admirable mission I supposed. There were a few unoccupied foxholes at the edge of the clearing where the guerillas lurked and the bulk of the company was apt to avoid. The privates and I dug up some more as quickly as we could so that all the men would have some shelter. We hunkered down with a cool breeze sending unnatural chills across my skin, staring into a wall of stirring jungle. I knelt my body low in the foxhole with Cerberus fitting snuggly beside me. Both our heads stuck up from the hole while we watched the jungle with the force of thirteen men doing the same on our adjacent flanks.

I placed my M1 Garand on the side of me, and pulled the Japanese light machinegun off my shoulder and relaxed for the first time today, leaning my back against the dirt and struggling to keep my eyes open. The wind was steadily picking up which only served to mask the movements of any IJA advance even more so than normal. The swaying wall of the Palmettos, Coconut Palms and lush vegetation was almost hypnotizing, and as much as I fought the urge to sleep, my eyes continued to grow heavier with the passing minutes, staring. After an hour or so, I was out cold, with my head tilted back against the dirt and more than likely in a steady snore as my muscles and brain gave in to the sweet temptation of sleep. I had no idea how much time had passed when a movement at my side snapped me out of my slumber. Cerberus stood high on his lanky back legs, he was agitated and stirred me awake in time to hear some rustling in the nearest patch of forest. I looked at the dog's eyes as they appeared luminescent against the abyss of darkness, and I easily recognized through his body language that the enemy was nearing. I signaled to my squad, as a few had to be awoken by their more vigilant comrades, and we aimed our weapons at the impending guerrilla warfare. I could see that Cerberus had his head and attention pulled to my left some, but I still pointed the reclaimed automatic trophy gun towards my right and waited. I placed my finger on the trigger as I heard the rustling in the low hanging branches once again, others heard it as well and leveled their weapons towards the same spot. We waited, ready, and after a few tense minutes of squeezing on the trigger, suddenly a small pig ran out of the brush and into the field oinking and rooting quietly. We all nearly shot at the tiny figure until it was apparent that it was no threat at all, and exhaled in near laughter.

Still I got the squad's attention again and signaled that the threat was still serious as I redirected them to the position where my watchful Doberman had never broken eye contact with. From there, it was a staring contest, each branch that swayed in the wind or blades of tall grass that stirred could be mistaken for a Japanese foot soldier moving ever closer to us in the surreptitious darkness. It began to play mind games with the men, anxiously waiting to shoot or be shot at by the Hetai. I scowled down the finned barrel of the foreign Type 99 Light Machinegun with the top fed thirty round curved clip blocking some of my view. I balanced the rifle against the earth with the bayonet attached to the gas block lying in the soft soil, and held my fire, almost painfully. That's when the Hetai burst forth from the exact location Cerberus had pointed us to, and charged our perimeter with no idea what they were up against. Our powerful M1918 BAR rifles and M1 Thompsons erupted in dazzling flashes in the night as I let off a torrent of rounds, strafing the hit and run guerillas with 7.7 x 5.8 mm Arisaka cartridges at a rate of seven hundred per minute. The group was a small contingent of brave warriors, but they mine as well have ran right into our barrels with how expertly our War Dog was able to locate them and predict their attack. Our Marines didn't let off the triggers, repelling them with automatic force as the majority of their hit squad collapsed to the ground before they could figure out what had gone so terribly wrong. It was difficult to see in the dead of night, a few had managed to return fire, and even fewer yet were able to escape the firefight when they had come to the realization that we had been ready and waiting for them the entire time. Feeling as though the Japanese weapon was returning retribution with every bullet it dispensed, I never let off the Type 99 LMG that Michael had been carrying when the punji stake booby-trap had impaled him. The rattling weapon was almost soothing as it finally emptied the clip and we realized that there were no more Japanese to shoot at as we effectively deterred the attack and more than likely even the thought of a counter attack with the war dog on site.

I tossed the empty Japanese LMG to the dirt next to the foxhole and retrieved my Garand to inspect the gloomy field up to forest's edge, but there were no more crazed soldiers charging to shoot at. Cerberus could hear the few survivors still running back through the bush as his ears twitched towards each indiscernible sound, until he relaxed some and just stared into the distance tirelessly, ever vigilant over his master and countryman. I thanked the amazing canine and offered him a snack from my pack which he gobbled up happily from my hand. My nap had recharged my body and the Japanese hit and run attack had rejuvenated my mind with a rush of excitement as we scrutinized the shadows, looking back out into the fatal jungle wilderness. One of the Privates on my nine hollered, 'Well that little plan didn't work so well for em, did it! Sent the nips runnin for the hills.' The rest of the men allowed themselves a moment of morale boosting laughter before again turning stern as we awaited another such sneak attack. After another hour or so, our sentry dogs showed up with a red Doberman and a German Shepard ready to take over our perimeter outpost. The dog handlers commended us for holding the fort until they showed, and relieved our men with a fresh squad so that ours could go to the center of the encampment to get some much needed and well-earned rest.

I was grateful to catch up on any sleep I could get as the stars glittered over us, but before I knew it the sun was casting a warm orange glow on my face as it crested the mountains. I blinked the light away and tried turning over in the uncomfortable pit of clay but I was too awake to fall back asleep. I opened my eyes and considered the early morning dew on the grass next to my head, the crickets chirped and the birds sang away in the forest as I stroked the sleeping Doberman and gave thanks just to wake another day. After a moment, I was up and pissing in a latrine before finding the supply tent where I filled my pack with 8 round en blocs as I loaded up on the .30-06 ammunition and grabbed Cerberus and I some grub. We were both starving and chowed down on the C rations consisting of canned goods already precooked. Most of the men were awake by now and gearing up for our next push into enemy territory. Major Davis found me and Cerberus shortly after our breakfast and applauded our efforts, 'That was some fine work in the defense of our Company last night.' He said, 'You must of set an example after repelling that last hit and run incursion, the IJA didn't try it again the rest of the night. Those war dogs are far more useful than I thought they'd be.'

'Yea, our Marine War Dogs were trained to do almost anything, they are extremely versatile, Sir. I'm just glad we averted any more casualties.' I answered.

Major Davis retorted, 'Not only did we avert any more casualties, your squad took out six Japs last night and I want you to get those confirmed kills Corporal. We also discovered some trails of blood headed back into the bush, appears we wounded some of them little shits before they fled.'

I replied indifferently, 'That's okay, spread those confirmed kills amongst the Privates, they earned them as much as me. There aint no telling who shot who out there last night. Really, that was nothing Sir… Cerberus is capable of far more than that.'

The gruff Commander stroked his grey goatee and grumbled, 'Now that's what I like to hear, we need more soldiers with that kind of attitude. You know something, I want to see exactly what your special scouting unit is capable of, let's get this Doberman Pinscher and you on point and see if we can infiltrate the IJA with their own game. I think I got just the mission for the two of you.'

Chapter 4

I was being drawn into the jungle by my enthusiastic scout dog from the edge of the field where I put him onto the blood trail that lay splattered in the grass. It may have been a half a night old, but the Doberman's nose had the scent as he dove into the forest and yanked me through the labyrinth of interlocked trees wrapped in dangling vines. As we parted ferns and stepped over the groves of thorny bushes, I spotted the droplets of blood speckled across the ground and painted against a giant fern in brownish red smears about waist high. Cerberus and I fell into a zone, obsessed with the tracking of our wounded foes, possessed with hunting down the enemy like a stalking tiger prowling its territory for a kill. We barely noticed our small support squad behind us as they exerted great effort to keep up with our movements. Cerberus and I were a team with a singular mind, my subconscious was connected to the dog in ways I could never fully fathom, innately or intuitively we just knew what the other was thinking. It wasn't the training that they drilled into us at the First War Dog camp, and it wasn't the battles that forced us into ever closer brushes with death. Although both helped raise our abilities to new limits, it wasn't what defined our bond. Our link went beyond even combat, to another stratosphere entirely. The Doberman Pinscher was an extension of me, a soldier and beast melded into a single killing machine, and as the dog pulled me after the guerillas down the blood laden trail, I swear I too, could also smell the blood.

The rainforest exuded a sweltering mist that floated in the air as the temperature soared higher, we were shoving our way through a tangle of undergrowth so thick it made every movement strenuous. Perspiration poured down our faces and arms and down our legs filling our boots. It was only growing more difficult the further into the interior of the jungle that we made it, with a proliferation of Coconut Palms sprouting under and over us. Our squad weaved between Ifit trees and Tangan Tangan thickets all while barbed bushes scraped our arms and legs with spiny branches. We plunged into a hidden creek in the mass of vegetation that was thigh deep, and clawed up the mucky sides pulling the parasitic leaches off our skin once we made it out of the stagnant water. Cerberus didn't slow in the least, the thorns brushed against his coat harmlessly and his massive paws stomped the vegetation out of his away effortlessly. No hesitation, he just kept his nose on the trail like a bloodhound while he examined our surroundings simultaneously. I was able to let my mind wander and simply followed the grueling path of our demanding scout dog up the hilly tropical forest after the guerillas from the night before.

Our U.S. Marines were learning on the fly just how desperate the Imperial Army was as well as how adept they were at defending the tropical island. The invasion had placed the beachheads as deep as two thousand yards by nightfall, but the price for that mile of jungle had been steep, hundreds upon hundreds of our young men, many teenagers even, didn't make it past the opening day of combat. No one wanted to see that many coffins packed with young American boys being shipped off to their parents and loved ones for a closed casket funeral and nothing but a crisply folded flag to show for all their efforts. The superiors wanted us to make a fast charge into the enemy held territory with the bulk of our Division and some artillery support, but they didn't want any more surprises that would stall out our hard fought momentum and lose any more Marines than we had to. The last thing Major Davis wanted was to get his Company stuck in the jungle and get bogged down with the IJA ripping them apart with their lethally proven, irregular warfare. The answer to all the Lieutenant's problems was the War Dog Recon Unit recently attached to his company, and Davis felt he had the perfect weapon at his disposal to unleash on the Japanese. Thus he sent us out ahead of the Company with a small seven man squad and ordered us to find the path of least resistance as well as figure out where the enemies' fortifications were. The Major had instructions to hold the post for reinforcement Platoons as well as armor and artillery to arrive, though moving the latter through this rough terrain was unmanageably sluggish. It appeared that the Commanding General Turnage wanted to make his position into a forward outpost base of operations as a communication hub and supply center, so that our constant arrival of new soldiers would have a jump off point from which to continue the invasion.

Whatever the General's course of action would be on Guam, it was evident at this point that the Military War Dog Units would be at the forefront of the battle and perhaps the key to its liberation. I focused back on the task at hand as Cerberus snorted a snout full of trace odors in a patch of sprawling ferns. My team was built to be fast and quiet, and was composed of two fellow Snipers, two spotters armed with SMG's, and two marines for medium machinegun support. I liked our chances in a confrontation with my handpicked squad of experienced vets and tenacious hellhound sniffing out the enemy. After we trudged over the first few hills of vast tropical undergrowth, we found our way into the older rainforest where the giant Monkey Pod trees towered above us with their extensive network of long sprawling branches protruding and contorting like a complex maze of lush flora. The undergrowth was much easier to navigate as it grew sparser with the lack of sunlight able to penetrate the lofty canopy of colossal an ancient trees that dominated the landscape. The shade was pleasant but the gnats that buzzed around our faces were flustering, flying in our eyes and up our noses no matter how many times we swatted away the miniscule insects. The blood trail was still noticeable here and there, although it seemed that the survivors may have applied tourniquets to the wounded near the transition between the new and old jungle as we found less visible evidence of their movements now. It made no difference, the Doberman was so certain of his tracking that he rarely sniffed at the ground now and was in a full trot through the forest as we struggled to keep up with the animal.

I called for a short rest as the men tried to catch their breath and collapsed onto the giant exposed roots of the enormous trees. We sat for a moment in a circle, taking sips of water from our canteens and passing around a ration to snack on. Cerberus stood on guard, inspecting the jungle around the unit as a flock of Mariana Crows squawked at us in the branches above, their greenish black gloss of dark feathers dotting the branches to the tops of the tree. The dog's head tilted inquisitively at the birds as they continued their obnoxious squawks while we slapped at the mosquitos and nats swarming our faces and arms. After a few more minutes of respite, we got back under way in this prehistoric rainforest with our guns drawn and our eyes peeled. Cerberus was indicating to me that the IJA weren't far, we rounded a thick tree trunk and there in a patch of young, spikey, palm leaves, the scouting dog shoved his head in to smell. I pushed some of the broad triangular leaves aside which revealed a dash of red contrast against the green frond. The canine withdrew his head from the newly sprouted palm tree and stared at me right in my face, nose to nose as I smiled and praised his efforts while petting his head for a moment. We were on their heels twisting and turning around trees and masses of roots, stalking through the ancient forest with the reconnaissance team in hot pursuit of our prey and growing hungry for the kill. Then as Cerberus perked his head up and froze, the athletic beast signaled to the Japanese's position down into a deep ravine with an icy stare.

I looked back to the men and silently hand signaled to the whereabouts of the IJA as expressions of grimaced displeasure came over their faces. I knew what they were thinking, that steep gorge would be a trap with no way out for our few men if we ran into a major Japanese force and got caught up down there. But that was the burden of advanced recon, we were almost always outnumbered and on our own against whatever resistance we ran up against. These were courageous men, and against all the obvious dangers we descended the sharp incline down into the ravine. We crept along a rocky stream that cut the hillside in two, trying not to slip down the more vertical parts as we dropped lower into the valley of death. We helped each other on the slick rocks, trying not to falter on the unstable spots and allow a rock or two to fall down the hillside and signal our presence. After ten minutes or so, we had finally found flatter ground and once again picked up the pace as we snuck through the scenic beauty of the valley.

Perfume trees and Gingers blossomed with amazing aromas in a multitude of colored flowers ranging from light yellow to dark blue, the bees and vibrant butterflies buzzed from bloom to bloom with busy intent. The undergrowth had merged with overgrowth and created the thickest part of the forest yet as we crawled through the crevices and nooks behind our canine leader. Eventually we came to the east side of the ravine where a gorgeous waterfall plummeted in white sheets off a limestone cliff into a clear pond. The Lilly pads swayed from the waves of the waterfall and we could see fishing poles set up on the side of the pond. Then as Cerberus signed to the enemy we had been searching for, we found a well hidden assembly of huts pressed against the overhanging foliage around the pond. There were buried bunkers established on both sides of the pool in which Palm trees had been cut down and stacked with rocks and dirt piled on top to conceal Heavy Machinegun nests. I spotted a Type 3 Ho-Ni tank destroyer, the self-propelled 75 mm artillery gun was stationed near a dirt road with a squad of Hetai standing all around it in conversation. On the edges of the forest, I detected guard towers holding Snipers and heavy machineguns looking over the entire complex. The towers were constructed of bamboo that had become overgrown with camouflaging vines and the roofs were furnished with a fresh covering of palm leaves that were changed daily, presumably. It looked like a fishing village taken over and turned into a solid encampment of at least a hundred Japanese, but after I sent our youngest Sniper into the most climbable tree near us to get a look, he came down with his jaw hanging open. Nate, the young marksman with a thin mustache said, 'There's got to be at least two more of these encampments in this valley to the southwest, and I think there's a large battery on the eastern ridge overlooking the entire canyon.'

I withdrew my binoculars and looked to where he had pointed, and sure enough I made out the barrels of heavy artillery and what even looked like a tank or two. The southern ridge side was higher than the north side where the waterfall ran from, and the particular region where the Imperial Army had placed their big guns was an elevated patch of mountainous jungle. That heightened altitude meant those cannons could control the entire ravine for miles in either direction as well as much of the surrounding hills. I exclaimed, 'Shit, they got enough firepower on that ridge alone to light up a couple mile diameter, and I'm sure this friggen valley is crawling with Hetai.'

The Marine Sniper Nate said, 'Yea, and the other encampments look bigger too. This is a bad place to be… Real bad.'

I commanded him, 'Keep your cool, we're alright. We just got to be quick and try to get out of here without a sound.'

The Sniper looked on nervously, reiterating, 'I know we're on a recon mission Corporal, but the Japs are all over in the jungle, they're teeming in this gorge here. It's just not smart to be here is what I'm saying.'

'Jesus Christ, you don't think I know that.' I spouted, 'Every minute here is a chance that we get taken prisoner and have our fingernails peeled off, or have bayonet blades driven through our guts, so while we're nice and comfortable here private, let's just do what we came to do. Then we'll get the hell out on my say so.'

Dan, the middle aged machine gunner with the spare tire spoke up apprehensively while shaking his head, 'I'll be damned if we didn't find what the Major sent us out here to find.'

Then one of the spotters offered, 'Well those injured IJA led us right into their stronghold, thanks to you and your dog Sir.'

I told him, 'Don't mention it. Now let's get some coordinates and figures, who's got the maps?' We stayed towards the southern side of the ravine and tried to get some idea of how convoluted the defenses in the area were. From the shrouded concealment of the foliage, we worked our way to the southwest following the edge of the valley the whole way. We identified four independent fortified encampments along the length of the rift, the first three in similar resemblance and each holding approximately a hundred plus soldiers. The last encampment however was more like a bustling town, encircled in concrete buttresses with three Type 89 I-Go medium tanks and a fourth multi-turreted Type 95 heavy tank on the perimeter as well as what appeared to be a large field hospital at its center. This compound was more than twice the size of the others and held hundreds of men, maybe up to four or five hundred at this fortress alone. The buildings were less hut like and more permanent here, and the guard towers were erected higher than the trees. This was a major command post for the Imperial Army, and they were sending out and receiving Platoons of men at a constant rate. We also took notice of the garrison squads that they sent into the valley boundaries to do security sweeps from one encampment to the next. If we were discovered by just one of the thousand or so soldiers here, then we were all dead, simple as that.

As we got done surveying the stronghold at the end of the ravine, we began trekking back northeast after a thorough scouting of the entire area. My men were filled with angst and we were all on edge with the hordes of infantry all around us, literally standing in the enemies lair. Then as we passed the third encampment, a squad emptied from the barracks there and over twenty Hetai began their patrol duty, fanning out from their bunkers and scanning the forest for signs of infiltration. We jogged back from the compound's edges as quiet as humanly possible, an after getting caught and fighting frantically in a tangle of Strangling Fig vines, we all dove for cover under the surrounding plant life and held our breaths. Several of the foot soldiers meandered past us, doing their sweep with machineguns pointed and heads swinging side to side. I hid under a sprouting palm tree, pressing against the spikey trunk and pulling Cerberus as far under the fronds with me as I could. I hadn't had time to see where the rest of my crew had managed to hide, I just hoped it was good enough to not be spotted. Then, thankfully the soldiers had passed us without ever suspecting that they had been walking right on top of a recon team. We reappeared from the thick foliage and got back on task, all sweating a little more than usual.

We neared the midway point of the valley and fixed our attention to the mountainous cliffs on the southern side. The real problem with all this Japanese activity was the Howitzers and Mortars they had stockpiled on the mountain crest. The IJA knew their barracks and stronghold were safe with the overlooking artillery outpost maintaining control of the vast swaths of territory around them, and they built up men and arms accordingly here in the protected valley. We tried to get a visual of the artillery battery on the ridge, but being directly underneath it allowed us to only view the oversized barrels jutting out from the cliff side, looking down ominously over the surrounding jungle. I hurriedly jotted down the coordinates of the battery and got ready to set out for the eastern entrance and begin the climb up the stream from which we had come down, when Cerberus snapped to attention back on our six. We couldn't hear it yet, but there was something headed our way and there was getting to be too many soldiers out here for us to keep in order. My men looked at me for direction as my brain felt scrambled from the heat and exhaustion as the pressure mounted on top of every neuron firing on overdrive, the stress of combat continuously pushing and overworking the interlaced dendrites networking my thoughts together. I knew we couldn't rush ahead too far as that line of IJA would be just in front of us, but we obviously had new troop movement closing from the rear in a hurry.

Not knowing how close the original sweep of Imperial infantrymen was to the west, I nonetheless decided to move slowly in that direction because sitting around waiting to be found didn't seem to be a great idea either. I didn't want to get pinched between the two lines of Japanese, so I told my men to move east with extreme caution and to find the best concealment we could manage. The sweep coming from our west was moving with a much brisker pace than anticipated, and we could hear them crashing through the branches behind us. My men looked panicked stricken as I gave the hand signal to take cover with them closing to less than a hundred feet. The overweight machine gunner dove under some Tangan Tangan brush on my right, our sniper and spotter crawled behind a log and pulled decaying leaves over their bodies. My other spotter embedded himself in bushes full of bright red choke berries while the last man followed me towards a thick expanse of undergrowth. I fell back into a bed of giant ferns whose broad leaves ended in still unwinding spirals. I hand signaled for Cerberus to crawl over to me and lay in steady silence, no matter what. The Doberman did so with a decent coverage of sprawling ferns over him and settled down in an obedient stillness just as I began to hear the footsteps of the Hetai. There were more in this sweep than the last, and at no more than fifty feet away they came through the jungle with a brashness, slicing up dense branches with jabs from their bayonets and zig zagging in random twist.

The line was about twenty feet away and we were all lying flat on the ground, gambling with our lives that they simply continued their sweep unaware of the small team of Americans hiding in their occupied ravine under all their guns and noses. We stayed buried in the foliage scared stiff, and while we waited a large millipede crawled from the wet dirt up my shoulder and for some damn reason scuttled towards my neck as a Japanese infantryman stepped past me in the clearing of ferns. I watched his tarnished boots land two yards from my head while the repulsive pest began creeping across my face with its thousand prickling feet crawling from my chin to my cheek, the pincers and antennas feeling over my skin as the hair raised up on the back of my neck. The boots paused there for a moment as I thought about anything but smacking the gross irritant from my face as its segments writhed and wiggled about. I could see the fraying laces and scratches in the leather as he kept listening and scanning around the forest, then finally they began to take slow steps, continuing the patrol march. The greyish brown segmented bug had finally found its way off my face while I still held my breath and watched it scuttle on and disappear under a rock.

More searching combatants did the same, pushing aside tall springs of grass with their feet or prodding inside thick bushes with their barrels and then moving on to the next bush or overgrowth of braches to inspect. An older soldier stopped next to the bush with the bright red berries and looked hard at it for a few seconds. I knew we had a man in that bush, the Japanese soldier standing over him with only his waist and the clip feeding his machinegun in view from under the spore covered undersides of the concealing fronds. The man seemed interested in something, and moved his hand towards the bush as I realized that all hell was about to break loose. Then he grabbed one of the berries and pulled it off the stem and popped it in his mouth before making a bitter face and moving on in his patrol. I bet my spotter was shitting bricks under that bush I thought to myself, trying to suppress laughter from just thinking about it. A few more advanced past us on our sides and it looked as if the coast was clear.

Just as I was about to begin crawling out from my secluded position, Cerberus pawed hard at my leg causing me to stop and look back at him. A few seconds later I heard it, the straggler who was bringing up the rear. He stumbled through the thickets, trying to catch up to his line from the looks of it. I crawled back under the fern another foot or two and froze back into a barely breathing rock of human flesh, trying my utmost to assimilate into the natural environment. The last soldier was double timing past the ferns, past the log with our men hiding under molting leaves, and then when he was almost out of view the youthful man stumbled to one knee before recovering. He turned confused, looking perplexed at the thickets he had crossed as if he should have seen a large root or rock that had caught his foot. Instead he noticed a polished boot under a branch, he pushed back the leafy branches of the Tangan Tangan saplings with the menacing barrel of his Type 38 Arisika and his eyes went wide. Our chubby machine gunner Dan was staring down the barrel of the bolt action rifle that was about to blow his head off and alert the entire IJA of our existence behind their lines. The startled infantryman began to shout, 'Sono Amerikahito…' as his finger slipped from the trigger guard to the curved piece of slender metal and as he began to pull it, I plunged my buck knife into his throat, driving the blade with all my strength while putting him in a headlock with my free arm and my bicep muffling his first words. The long steel blade sank into his soft esophagus without resistance, stifling the soldier while I gripped hard on the mahogany handle. The razor edge continued into his vocal cords and carotid with some extra force, as I ripped the brutal instrument towards his jugular vein and carotid artery and then yanked it out with a twist of the wrist devastating the wound more so. Blood ran down his front in surging liters of volume and sprayed on my arm still locked around his head. I gently and ever so slowly dropped the convulsing soldier to the thickets at Dan's side, and angrily motioned for the dumb bastard to cover the kid up with branches and leaves immediately. God how I wanted to kick Dan in the fucking teeth as hard as I could for nearly getting us all killed with his mistake, but I kept my composure while I looked on. The Japanese man still moved and gasped, but only the gurgling of a red river gushing from his slit throat was truly heard, he was dead, he just didn't know it yet.

I replaced my drenched knife to its sheath at my belt and watched as the nearly dead IJA combatant was covered in brush and grass, with Nate offering help and trying to cover up the blood by laying leaves over the heavy splashes on the ground. I got us reorganized and ready to go out while I picked up Cerberus' leash as he prepared to extract us from the ravine as securely as only he could. Then I noticed the blood stain on the leash's loop that I held, and looked down at my hands, painted in the life sustaining substance of the young soldier. The man whose life I had ripped away like a raptor diving on unsuspecting prey and snatching it in his talons, ripped away like the grim reaper himself. The vivid red fluid collected on my palms in chilling pools, the blood was under my fingernails and ran down my wrist and forearms. I attempted to clean my hands on my fatigue pants but to no avail, the blood only smeared some with the majority still caught on my palms. The men all looked at me with a new found respect, there was almost a fearful way about them it seemed after witnessing the slaying. But at the same time they were as grateful as ever, it was war and they knew it. I despised war, but I didn't let the death weigh on my conscience in that valley as I started leading them towards the stream egress, not when it was kill or be killed.

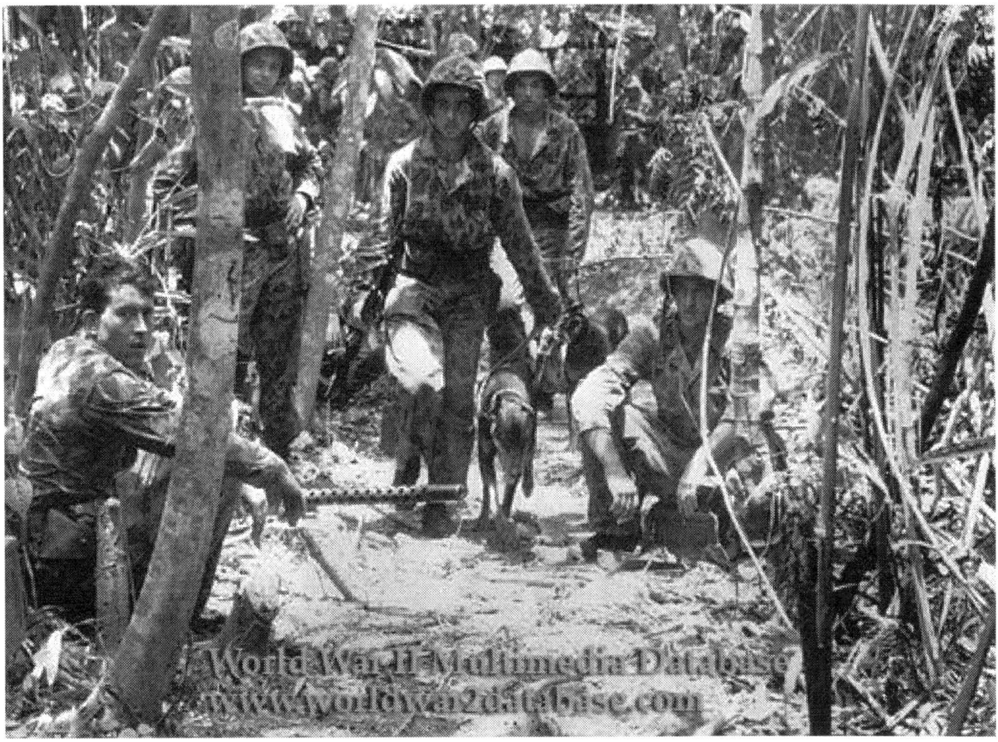
World War II Multimedia Database
www.worldwar2database.com

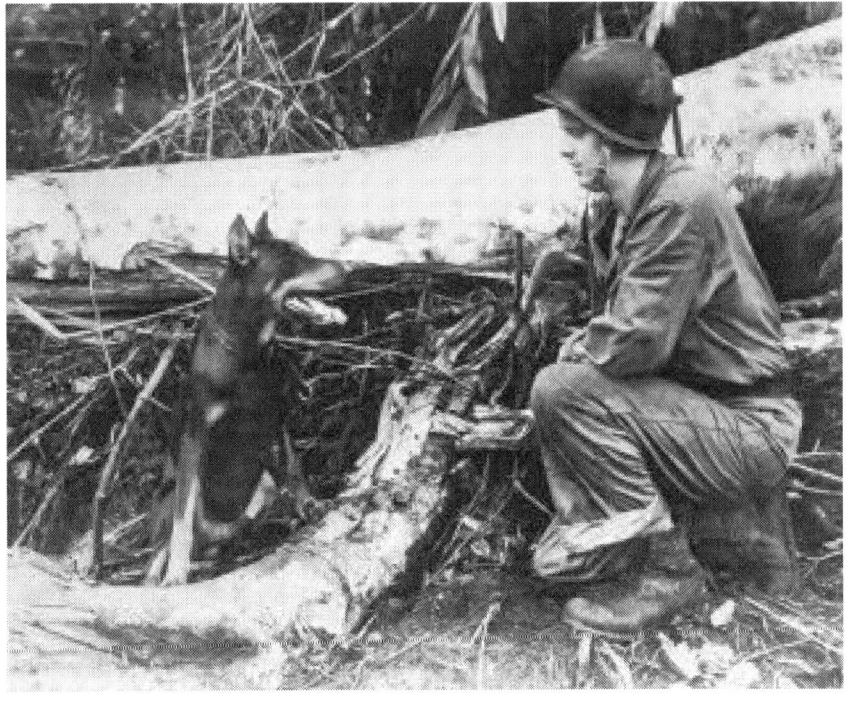

Chapter 5

Cerberus led the squad back to the base, but by the time we made it to our lines the sun had already set. Once back from where we had started earlier in the day, we were amazed to see the transformation of the encampment into a fully barricaded base with armor in the form of M4 Sherman Medium tanks at the corners as well as HMGs at the entrances on the north and south of the growing installation. Thick walls of dark earth standing nearly ten feet high had been freshly bulldozed all around the perimeter, providing security to those inside. We passed the guards manning the M2 Browning 50 BMG, the soldiers nodded in appreciation as if they had been expecting us. Once inside the compound I took notice to the temporary tin buildings that had been erected in one corner for the commanders and supplies. There was also a large expanse of olive green tents covering more than half the base that provided barracks for the men, although there were still plenty of open foxholes being occupied by slumbering soldiers. The bustling compound paused as their attention was transfixed onto our ragged and exhausted squad walking in, trying to get our bearings. A Sergeant approached us with others behind him, as they congratulated us on our return and began asking questions or telling us the developments. Some of them even mocked Cerberus and ridiculed what the hell the Marines were doing running around the jungle with a glorified mascot. Rather than punch the less refined jokers in the face and start a scuffle, I ignored them and moved on towards the tin buildings where we were directed by an Officer to the Command Center to meet with Commanding Officer Robbert Frank and Major Davis to be debriefed.

Upon entering the makeshift shack with its large map of Guam rolled out flat on a table with symbolic pieces placed around it representing troop counts and naval ships, I was greeted with a warm handshake from the the Major. Several of the other men were brought to different quarters for debriefing while the rest were dismissed. Davis introduced me to Commanding Officer Lieutenant Colonel Frank and a group composed of three Staff Sergeants, a Gunnery Sergeant, and a Second Lieutenant. They listened intently to what our advanced reconnaissance was able to find, all the while Cerberus sat dutifully at my side regarding the high ranking meeting with disinterest. I pointed to the map while expressing caution as I illustrated my findings, explaining that the bombing raids from the prior weeks had forced vast numbers of soldiers into the narrow and deep ravine as it provided shelter from our twin engine B-25 Mitchells as they dropped their payloads on any target they could locate. Major Davis was thrilled with the intelligence gathered, but the Lieutenant Colonel was devoid of emotion as he listened, the man seemed to have the warmth of a glacier. He asked, 'So then why shouldn't we march our battalion to the northern cliffs and shell the shit out of the encampments with heavy artillery til' we kill every nip in the valley?'

I stated, 'We located a well hidden artillery battery on the higher ridge on the southern side, and upon further surveillance from the northern cliffs on our way out, I was able to make out a powerful arsenal of Type 4 Rocket Launchers, Mortar teams, an what looks to be a combination of 7 cm Mountian Guns, 28 cm Howitzers L/10s, an Type 45 Howitzers. And...' I hesitated for a moment.

The Commanding Officer, Colonel Robbert Frank asked, 'Is that it soldier?'

I replied, 'I believe they are even equipped with German weapons, such as Anti-Aircraft 12.8 cm Flack Twin 40's and most disturbingly a piece of superheavy seige artillery, what could in my oppinion only be 42 cm Gamma Morser Howitzer, it was assembled into the side of the mountain using overhanging rock ledges as cover. They also undoubtedly have a secret network of tunnels and caves connecting the valley encampments to the cliffside battery and hidden bunkers throughout the southern mountain, it is a hell of a fortress, Sir.'

Some of the lower Officers looked shocked at this revelation, one tried to suppress a gasp from leaving his mouth. The Officers looked intrigued as the Gunnery Sergeant blurted out, 'Fascinating, the Nazis inniatiated secret weapon deals with the Japanese to help bolster their efforts, makes you wonder what else was going on between the two nations. I truly hope the Luftwaffe didn't let the IJA get their hands on any of those advanced Henschels, or state of the art Enzian missiles for that matter.'

Major Davis said, 'Shit, looks like the Germans were supplying the Imperial Army with some of their best equipment to refortify the Pacific front of the Axis powers. Does the OSS know about this?'

Commanding Officer Frank recounted, 'I had heard some theories from our Intelligence agencies about a possible trade between the two superpowers several months ago, but if this Recon Scout is correct, than this is the first evidence of such a transaction.' If I impressed the man with the intelligence I gathered from my scouting observation, he didn't show it, besides for maybe a a quick smirk through his cold, tight lipped demeanor. 'I'll have to inform Admiral Conolly and General Geiger on the command ships about this development... Those Gammas have a range of three miles, and that's on flat ground, I can only imagine the range from up on that mountainside.'

I replied, 'Yea, the Japanese Commanders weren't slow to react to the suspected invasion, they fortified that mountain knowing our bombardment would force their troops to seek shelter in the ravine. It appears that instead of breaking their morale, we have only driven them underground and into the most fortified positions from which to defend.'

Major Davis exclaimed, 'That was good work Corporal, phenomenal job, incredible what you and your dog were able to do. I believe you gathered more intelligence back beind their lines in a single day then the most advanced spy planes have in the last month.' He let out a hearty laugh and slapped me on the shoulder which caused

Cerberus to snap his head up and eye the Officer suspiciously, at least until I chuckled back leading my furry guardian to relax.

Lieutenant Colonel Frank replied, 'Indeed, you kept us from quite a disasterous ambush had we stumbled into that valley with our pants around our ankles trying to uproot those Japanese bases.' He marked on the map as he went on, 'So this is where all those reserve troops keep coming from to fortify Fonte Hill and the Mount Tanjo. It appears this sector is the command and communication hub for the IJA's organized defenses of the 48th mixed regiment and 10th brigade in the central part of the island, and the sooner we disable them here, the quicker we can get them on the run, although this task will be much more difficult then I anticipated if the stockpile of artillery is as you say. Apparently our preliminary bombings didn't weaken them as much as the Admiral Conolly had foreseen, but nonetheless we now know where to attack and more importantly where to avoid. I will make note of this to my superiors, it appears there is quite a vital role that your War Dogs may play in this liberation.'

I thanked him for his words, as Davis exclaimed to the Colonal, 'I told you Sir, this could be the future of land warfare with US infantry reconnaissance. I believe the Corporal and his Doberman are perfect for the mission in the southwest near the Ylig river.' He then directed his energetic speech to me, 'We are in a race against time son, and only the Lord knows how many lives weigh in the balance.'

Lieutenant Colonal Frank interjected gruffly, 'Yes, there is quite an important mission you may be perfectly suited for, but that is classified at the moment and is on a need to know basis. Perhaps if and when we break these Jap lines of resistance here at the beachheads, then we will assign the Corporal to that mission, but until that time, that will be all.'

I saluted the Officers before being dismissed so that they could devise strategies moving forward and so we could get some sleep. It appeared the Commanding Officer understood what kind of hell was awaiting our men out there in the mountains, but he just didn't seem to care. I couldn't help but notice the way Officer Frank looked at Cerberus and I, as though he wasn't looking at anything more than a new weapon he had discovered. It was apparent that the workload of assignments we were tasked with was only going to come faster and grow more dangerous in the days to come. Yet at the moment, all I wanted to do was find my tent and pass out on a firm bunk to relax my back and aching feet. As I set my pack on the ground and my M1 rifle under the cot, I laid down while my Doberman did the same on the soft dirt right next to me as I fell into a vast darkness as I closed my eyes.

That night I jumped to my feet as the earth trembled, reaching for my Garand and rushing out through the fabric walls barefoot as I tried to get my bearings in the confusion. Over in the nearest corner of the base from which I could see, there was a twenty foot section of scattered bodies and burning tents, then I watched as another 50 mm High Explosive Mortar shell fell from the skies and detonated near the first shot. The soil erupted from the wall in a thirty foot high cloud of debris and smoke, as shrapnel whistled through the air while it sliced into everything in its path. The shockwave sent more men flying from where they had slept, tossed from their tents with combustible explosions shredding them open and catching the nearby tents ablaze. The deafening blast left only the sound of a high pitched ringing in my ears, as yet another detonation sounded, although thankfully this volley had fallen short and just behind the compound walls. MP's and medics rushed the scene where the first two Mortars had struck, and outside the compound the sounds of our Sherman medium tanks firing back their massive 75 mm tank guns and .30 caliber secondary armaments towards where the mortar fire seemed to have been hailed was filling the night with the reverberations of war. I started to move towards the chaos and mayhem before a small Army jeep rode past and a line of men cut me off, telling everyone it was under control and to return to our barracks. I was stunned but realized that the medics and doctors were really the only ones that could help those unfortunate souls now, so I took Cerberus back to our tent. As I laid back down, I tried to block out the 50 caliber machine guns bursting off outside the walls and tried not to think of one of those Mortar rounds landing directly on top of my sleeping quarters, shredding my body into pieces in over a hundred foot diameter, like had happened only a short distance away, merely minutes before. I realized that it was just another night in Guam, and somehow laughed as I actually envied the soldiers who were sleeping in one of those uncomfortable foxholes. I wondered if this war was getting to me as I fell back asleep, only from pure exhaustion.

As I awoke in the morning, I realized I had made it to D-day plus 2, and I also found my large dog sleeping on top of me like a puppy, no longer content to sleep on the ground, making it a struggle to get his hefty mass off of me as I tried to roll out of bed. Cerberus jumped up behind me when he seen me put my boots on, I was starving and led the way out of the tent and into the center of this new swelling base. The smell of burning tents was still smoldering in the northern corner, and I could see engineers trying to rebuild the wall with a camo painted Bulldozer and fill in the craters so as to set up more tents for our arriving troops from the sea. I wondered if any of the Marines that had been within the blast radius of those Japanese Mortars had survived through the night on those cold surgery tables in the makeshift OR.

I found my way to a latrine with some barrels of water, quickly washing up and shaving as the sun had just begun to rise. I was drawn to a firepit in the middle of the encampment where some A-rations were smoking over a bed of glowing coals. There was a large boar being roasted on a stake, slowly spinning. My mouth watered at the thought of something fresh for a change, the stale, dry, precooked C-rations could barely be considered food and tasted like cardboard. I was served a heaping pile of a prime cut from the roasting boar, and as more Marines awoke, they took notice of the oddity Cerberus and myself presented, with the Doberman walking freely around our encampment as I rarely leashed him anymore. We retreated to our tent and scarfed down the delectable cuts of juicy pork and awaited orders in the shade of the tent while I field stripped my rifle for a thorough cleaning. At 0800 hours, a Staff Sergeant visited us at our quarters interrupting a letter I was writing, he informed me of direct orders from Major Davis that we would be heading southwest and back to the coast to a village called Piti. The Staff Seargent spoke through narrow eyes and too authoritatively for my liking, repeating the chain of command, 'You and that dog will catch a ride on a half-track back that way in fifteen minutes, and regroup with the 21st Outfit, and from there you will lead a Rifle Company to Piti before the raid. From our arial images, the small coastal village seemed to be crawling with the IJA, so your Advanced Scouting Unit is to lead the point, the Colonel and Major want no surprises on this one, and no more delays.'

On the back of the M5 half-track, the breeze flew through our stuffy gear at a brisk 25 mph on the bumpy roads, and the morning sun rose ever higher, slowly raising the humidity of our tropical paradise. The half-track had the tracks of a tank combined with the front end of a transport truck, on top of its flatbed was mounted a M2 BMG 50 cal. and riding with us on the open back were 12 other troops and a bunch of disassembled M2 Mortars. They stared at me intently, but mostly at Cerberus with wide eyes, some looked impressed and others a little nervous. The first twenty minutes of the ride were devoid of so much as a whisper until one of the Marines finally asked, 'Is it true that you and your dog killed ten Hetai behind enemy lines with your bare hands?'

Though the effects of war had begun to create a somber mood within my mind as I reflected on the events thus far, I found myself laughing at the question. I stopped laughing with all the men's attention on me and said, 'No, I don't recall that ever happening. Who told ya that tale?'

The young kid with a shaved head and a babyface said, 'I don't know, it was a chubby guy, I think his name was Don... Or maybe it was Dan. Something like that.'

'It was Dan, that bastard is always talkin!' I shouted over the low drone of the diesel motor.

He said, 'Yea that's it, but anyways he said he saw it himself with his own eyes.'

I shook my head and replied, 'I can't say that I've ever killed a man with my bare hands, although Cerberus here has probably slain at least that many with that big grinning mouth fulla teeth.' The kid who had been leaning in to conversate now regarded the happy dog with his glimmering jagged molars and prominent canines on full display as he panted in the heat. He quickly scooted backwards a few feet against the base of the M2 BMG and kept a close eye on the growing legend that the Doberman was amassing.

Another one of the Privates leaned over to me and shouted with a strong Boston accent, 'Sorry, this is most of ours first action, my name is Nathan, Sir.' I nodded at the youngin, he also had a closely shaven head and a cheerful attitude, but I knew it wouldn't be long before the war took that smile off his face. He continued, 'This is the first time our Mortar team has been off the ship and in the action.'

I replied curtly, 'I'm sure you will be seeing plenty of action soon enough.'

He nodded eagerly at the proposition, then Nathan asked, 'So what's your dog's name?'

I told him, 'His name is Cerberus, he's a Doberman Pinscher and the best scout I've ever worked with in the military.'

Nathan said, 'Yea I can tell, beautiful dog. Does his name mean something or..?'

'Cerberus' I yelled, 'He's named after the mythical Greek hell hound. According to the mythology, Cerberus was a giant three headed dog that guarded the gates to the underworld, only letting souls pass through and devouring any living flesh that tried to enter the gates.'

The kid said, 'That is wild, Sir. Seems like a fitting name.'

I responded, 'You have no idea, this dog has been guarding the literal gates of hell here on Guam the way only an ungodly beast could.' I sighed and then Cerberus put his head on my shoulder trying to get me to pet him, and as I scratched his ear the dogs back leg kicked wildly in appeasement. And while I scratched the left side of his head, I checked the military tattoo they branded on the inner skin of his triangular ear. The tattoo read T475 in black ink, the Doberman Pinscher had been marked as top secret property of the US government a long time ago. A while later, we came around a bend in the road and to our shock the M5 half-track swerved and decelerated as it nearly slammed into the smoldering remains of one of our Sherman tanks, charred up and black from thin smoke plumes that still faintly rose from its many fissures. The tracks were tore from the base and there was a large hole of warped and twisted metal in the rear of the medium armored tank. Not more than another hundred feet there was another M4 Sherman that had been eviscerated, this wreckage worse than the last with the huge 75mm tank gun bent at an acute angle and the side hull missing so much steel that I could literally see inside the tank cabin where the inside compartment still smoked. I took in the surroundings, such as the brownish blood trails leading from the hole where the victims had been pulled out from, and how the blast seemed to have originated from underneath the armored goliaths as the fractures climbed upwards in the steel frames.

Finally a few short moments later, after about an hour total, we had reached our destination on the side of a road leading into Piti. The road was obstructed with deep tank trap holes excavated, and other sections of road were blocked where Coconut trees had been cut down and laid out in stacks for a dozen yards at a time. It was here we would begin our next journey into enemy territory, as I was hurried from the half-track by some rambunctious Privates to meet with First Lieutenant Slater. The Company leader Slater looked pissed off, he was in his thirties and puffing anxiously on a cigarette as he paced in circles. While wounded men from his outfit were loaded onto the back of the M5 half-track, he stared me down silently for a few moments before flicking away a cigarette butt and lighting a new one with his Zippo. Finally he briefed me on their issues and my objectives, offered me a smoke which I waved off, and started setting up his formation, placing me up front as the point and ordered me to avoid the road to Piti at all cost. The reason they had requested that a War Dog Scout Unit be attached to spearhead the push to take Piti was due to a complete debacle from the prior evening. The Lieutenant warned me about the anti-tank mines that halted their armor push and described the expertly maneuvered roadside ambushes that turned his Company inside out. It was also his understanding that the village was empty of all native Guam people and Piti had been retrofitted into an Imperial Army stronghold. As I looked for a suitable route to traverse on one of my maps, I noticed many of the men were involved in a prayer circle taking place, asking God and the brothers they had lost the day before to watch over them as they continued the mission.

I looked at Cerberus who was already tugging on his leash towards the nearest wall of foliage, and told the men nearest to me, 'Their prayers have been answered today, this dog is all the protection they could ask for.' The two men looked up from the collection of maps in their hands and tried to force a smile, but I could see the nerves and fear in their eyes. It was time to get these boys out of the Japanese kill zone, I unclipped Cerberus from his harness and set out into the jungle not far behind him. The Rifle Company set out in line and followed our path, getting off the hazardous entrapments of the road and being swallowed into mothernature herself. Cerberus was at a trot when I had to signal for him to slow down so we didn't lose the rest of the Marines. Some of the poor bastards were lugging heavy machine guns and mortar parts, and it was exponentially more difficult marching off the roads, but invariably safer.

The village wasn't far from our starting point, though we were taking a winding path along a stream bed that led just outside the town. It didn't take long before Cerberus located guerillas moving towards the road in the Guinea grass and Tangan Tangan thickets on the opposite side of the creek. They glided like animals through the forest, their movements smooth and nearly soundless. I froze the men with a hand gesture and called up from the huge column of Marines behind me for some HMGs. From within our cover of tall Guinea grass, brush, and Banana Palms, Cerberus pinpointed the squad of Hetai directly across the streambed. I followed the direction of his long snout straight ahead to a dense patch of bush with my binoculars, in which I was able to peep the occasional glint of a polished bore through the crevices of leaves, or a arm just slightly bend a thin branch of a small tree. There was absolutely no way anyone would have seen that squad of Imperial veterans moving so fluidly, not without the extraordinary senses of our brave canine. This was exactly the kind of squad that regularly ambushed our troops on previous island battles around the Pacific with hit and run guerrilla warfare that sent entire Rifle Companies into disarray and in full retreat for their lives. Except now the style of warfare had changed dramatically with our War Dog Platoon's activation, for Cerberus had smelled the scent of these hardened Japanese troops before we ever left the road and stepped foot into the rainforest.

Due to the Hetai's adept movements, I couldn't be sure how many there were, so I lined up a squad with automatic weapons, and the six teams of soldiers wielding Heavy machineguns were ordered to spray enfilading fire from the outside of the enemy formation to the center, from both the left side and right respectfully. The two man teams of machine gunners quickly assembled their Browning M1919A4s onto their tripods, with the gunners taking aim and the assistant gunners feeding in the 250 round woven cloth belt of .30 caliber ball cartridges. The gunners began to pull back the cocking handles and released them so the bolt of the extractor claw grabbed ahold of the first cartridge and slammed it forward, '*Click.. Clack*'. The Lieutenant Slater gave the signal to take aim and the gunners pulled back the handles a second time forcing the first round into the chamber while advancing a second round from the belt onto the clawed bolt extractor. I knew time was of the essence as the enemy combatants could quickly disappear back into the veil of vegetation and lose us our rare chance to ambush the ambushers. Lieutenant Slater looked to me as I scanned through my binoculars, dictating to the gunners that they were just over ninety yards out. They took aim with their fixed iron sights at the end of the dull perforated barrels and I gave a thumbs up to the Lieutenant. He nodded and told the HMG teams with an erratic whisper, 'Aim... Fire.' They pulled on the triggers releasing the spring-loaded firing pin to strike the primer of the cartridge, and the barrels exploded with gunpowder and bullets. Brass shell casings flew out of the ejector to the right of the weapons as the Marines used 5 second burst of fire, strafing the area of brush and trees that Cerberus had directed me to. The belts were guided out of their ammo box into the Brownings by the gunner assistants as the weapons ate through their belts at a rate of 1,200 rounds per minute. The trees and bushes were ripped apart where they had once stood, leaves fell in every direction, branches chopped down from Betal Nut trees, and thickets of Tangan Tangan were leveled flat. The foliage that had once enshrouded the Japanese was quickly reduced to mere patches of plant life, the buzzsaw of .30-06 rounds from the M1919 Stingers had sliced the entire squad of twelve men nearly in half. The line of perforated barrels flashed almost continuously as the belts were rapidly dragged out of the ammunition boxes into the heavy machine guns and the spent casings flung into the air by the hundreds while each gunner pivoted his M1919A4 monstrosity on its small tripod. No man could have escaped the ambush, with the overbearing firepower leaving nothing untouched, and after a solid minute of automatic strafing, I halted the gunners.

A few minutes later Cerberus silently brought me across the creek and close to the new clearing, I counted out twelve bodies of which only one was still breathing. It looked to be a Japanese Officer or some ranking infantry soldier, and I could hear his words slowly trail off from edge of the tore up ground littered with blood, weapons, corpses, and broken branches. The Officer or Sergeant grabbed his gashed open torso where blood soaked his uniform as it oozed by the liter, writhing in pain until I heard a final gasp. My perceptive Doberman gave no indication of survivors or any other enemies nearby, so we regrouped the Company and the column of Marines fell back in line once again, pushing through the lush oasis of Guam. We encountered two other smaller skirmishes as the IJA sent squads to investigate the sounds of gunshots, but the scout dog warned the Company of the foot soldiers at a minimum of 200 yards in each instance as we prepared and repelled them time and again. The key to guerrilla warfare was the element of suprise, it meant everything in the outcome of irregular combat, yet through my Doberman Pinscher I was able to locate, track, and even predict the IJA's movements to a deadly degree. Cerberus was single handedly thwarting every attempted attack by the enemy, and it usually cost them their lives for even trying. Without our scouting unit on the point leading the way, this mission would have taken days and lost our Marines countless bodies, but as it was, Cerberus had swiftly an almost effortlessly taken us to the edge of the forest near Piti within only a few hours with the entire Company unharmed. It would seem the Marine War Dog Platoon was revolutionizing combat in the Pacific in ways no one had ever expected.

At the edge of the coastal village, our scouting objective was completed and the Rifle Company now had the task of driving the IJA Garrison out of the town. Lieutenant Slater thanked me graciously, he was astonished at the difference a War Dog Scouting Unit could make to a mission. The deaths of his Marines and destruction of both the M4 tanks that were assigned to escort them to Piti had plummeted morale, and now he felt far away from the setbacks of only a day before. But in my mind the hard part for the Company was just about to begin with the transition from the concealing jungle and guidance of Cerberus to brutal and chaotic urban combat. The town looked like nothing more than rice paddies and huts from our low vantage point, yet I was able to discern multiple pill boxes on the perimeters all connected by straight walls of sandbags and boulders. Slater peered through his binoculars from behind a palm tree and I could see anxiety take form on his face. He voiced his concern quietly so that only I could hear, 'This mission has great significance Corporal. Do you know why we are here?' I shook my head no as he cleared his throat and went on in barely a mumble, 'We're here to take the Piti Guns...Word from the higher ups is that they have some big guns here, Vickers-type Model 3's to be specific.'

I sat on the ground resting my back against one of the palm trunks and with a sideways glance asked, 'What caliber?'

Slater came back, 'A hundred and forty millimeters, shoots up to ten miles too.'

'Woww...God damn Lieutenant.' I replied.

Then Slater said, 'Yea, and my superiors told me they got photographs from spy planes, they believe the IJA got three of them brutes all secured in this here town, and lucky for our boys who landed on the Asan beach, these guns weren't fully operational yet. No doubt they would have blown away our vessels and landing craft with these coastal guns, but the Admiral is getting worried the IJA are close to having the guns ready to fire on his fleet, and we don't want that. The Japs could sink any cargo ship, destroyer, or LVT that we try to send near the shore, hell even the battleships and Hornet carrier would be susceptible, and we can't have our supply lines getting cut off, that's what the Japs are depending on.' I listened to Slater's information, he nervously plucked at his mustache as he went on. 'So that's why they sent us down here with armor and an entire Rifle Company, they need us to take this town, and if we can't take it... Well then no matter what we have to take out those massive coastal guns one way or another. We can not, under any circumstances, let those guns become fully operational.'

The Lieutenant seemed to be confiding in me for a sense of reassurance, wondering what his next move should be. It seemed Slater wasn't used to having so many men under his command and such grave responsibilities as the consequences of failing this mission weighed on him. I bent my head around the tree to steal a glance at the consolidated village, and asked, 'Well, were the aerial photos able to gain the coordinates for the coastal guns?'

Lieutenant Slater said, 'Yea, the coordinates are um... uh 13 degrees 27' 43" North and 144 degrees 41' and 40" East.'

I stated, 'Best thing to do then is set up two Mortar teams and launch some of them Four-Dueces at em, have one team aim for those Vickers-type Model 3 140's and have the second team blast the shit out of the interior bunkers and fortifications. That way we can open a way into the town and the Company can storm the compound without getting repelled by the pillboxes, shit you may take out some of the Piti Guns before we even get in the village. I mean, that's just a suggestion, Sir.'

Slater seemed to agree with my assessment, and I could tell he appreciated having another hardened veteran's perspective around. He set out at once, giving orders to the Company and getting the men ready for the raid. Cerberus and I absorbed ourselves into the mature rice paddies, kneeling in the swaying green grains and sinking past my ankles into the muck and water, still we maintained visual on the town and the entrenched IJA. We sloshed through the mire, trying to find any weakness or traps that the crafty enemy could resort to, the resourceful Japanese seemed to always be trying out new and unorthodox ways to kill American G.I.'s. As I scanned through my M73 scope attached slightly to the left of the receiver on top of my M1 Garand, I found that Piti had become a Imperial Army citadel, a fortress with large walls pulled together of rocks, sandbags, and boulders forming a rudimentary square around the town. At each corner of this square was a concrete hexagonal shaped pillbox from which loomed a combination of menacing Type 3 Taisho 14 heavy machineguns and the upscaled Type 92 Shiki Kikanju heavy machineguns poking out from the loopholes in the concrete. The bunkers themselves were piled with sandbag after sandbag, even the roofs were covered, and they were filled with armed soldiers peering out across the rice paddies with an abundance of small arms as well as HMG support. They would undoubtedly mow our troops down from their protected positions if we didn't neutralize these bunkers full of Woodpeckers and Taisho machineguns first. Beyond the walls of the Imperial Army's village enclave, I could see nothing more from the low ground of the rice paddies. As far as where those Coastal Guns were, all I could guess was probably further towards the sea, but without being able to see into the compound, I truly didn't know.

I looked back to where the marsh merged to forest and seen my Marine counterparts had nearly finished assembling the rifled mortar tubes into the hydraulic monopods and base plates. With the squads taking aim, I knew the M2 Mortars were about to lob unholy hell upon the Japanese and I signaled my Doberman to lay low and watch the fireworks. The M2 teams aimed what had become affectionately known by our forces as the Goon Gun, due to their combustible 4.2 inch diameter Mortar shells which in appearance resembled giant bullets. They began to make last second calculations for the trajectory and coordinates of their shelling. The team closer to me was the squad I had traveled with down here on the back of the half-track. The M2's poked their wide barrels just out from the edge of the rainforest, and I could see Lieutenant Slater preparing to signal for the bombardment and assault. The wide barrels sounded off and recoiled on their hydraulic monopods as the charges were detonated, the Mortars shaking the soft ground under the firing teams as they volleyed the M3 high explosive (HE) shells packed with 3.63 kilograms of TNT towards their intended targets. At once the two pillboxes infront of us were enshrouded in wicked fireballs that quaked the very concrete foundations and the grand wall of sandbags and boulders in front of us were flattened with more explosions tossing the rocks and bags flying in all directions. Another set of explosions flashed further inside the village and from the treeline Marines let loose with Browning M1919 heavy machine guns while the Mortar teams reloaded their high explosive projectiles.

The Japnese immediately began to fire back across the rice paddies from the trenches behind the walls, and once the smoke cleared around the bunkers, they too shot in a panicked and frenetic response. Due to our concealed positions and having got the jump on the IJA, they could only strafe the vast fields of rice paddies and forest edges blindly with automatic fire in desperate search of where they had been struck from. Only five feet from Cerberus and I, a line of 6.5 x 50 mm Arisaka rounds from a Type 3 HMG randomly explored the rice paddies blasting the marsh and covering us with muddy water as it tore up the crop field past us while I shielded Cerberus with my body. Suddenly more Mortar shells were launched by our Marine teams and the pillboxes again were rocked with high explosives, this time leaving the northern bunker completely obliterated as it caved in on itself. The second volley had almost exclusively focused on the pillboxes, with the HE rounds enshrouding the bunkers in explosion after explosion, bringing a merciless hurricane of steel rain upon the stunned Japanese Imperial Army.

I watched as the Marines were gearing up to rush the weakened eastern barrier of the coastal base, and I gripped my M1 Garand and lifted my head just barely above the rice grains to witness the vigorous combat exchanges. After a third barrage from our hidden M2 Mortar batteries, our troops sprinted across the marsh as they attempted to storm the wounded fortress with her eastern defenses crippled and her soldiers discombobulated. I pivoted my rifle from the northern pillbox that was smashed to mere rubble and towards the southern pillbox to see that somehow more than half of the bunker survived the Mortar salvos and remained miraculously unscathed. About a quarter of the concrete structure had collapsed and the Type 3 Taisho 14 was in ruins, yet the Type 92 HMG continued to lay down burst of 7.7 mm Shiki rounds and was cutting down the opening lines of our Marines with ease. I centered my Garand in a single fluid motion with the crosshairs of my scope just above the helmet of the crazed IJA gunner as he screamed vehemently from behind his mounted weapon. I knew there wasn't time to adjust the reticles and trusted my instincts as I let off a .30-06 Springfield that ripped through the swaying grains at a supersonic velocity towards the tiny window in the bunker from which heavy automatic fire sliced through the battlefield. Before my M1 reloaded another round into the chamber, the Type 92 Woodpecker had seized firing and I could see my shot had rang true with the main gunner slumped over the HMG. I watched through the small loophole and waited as one of the assistant gunners threw his deceased comrade to the side and took up the controls of his powerful weapon. Without letting him get a single shot off, I laced the Hetai square in the sternum and observed as he clutched his chest in shock and slowly stumbled backwards into the bunker and out of my view.

I was buying our guys as much time as I could manage from my less than desirable position, exposed in the middle of a rice swamp. But I believed if I could just keep the Japs off that HMG for another minute or two and allow the Marines to get into the compound, then they could take that pillbox before it cut through our ranks any more than it already had. This time, from the pattern that had developed to the previous gunners, the next assistant gunner was in no rush to take up the helm of the weapon with sniper rounds finding the hearts of anyone near the loophole. I shot another round at the empty window as it harmlessly ricocheted off the machine gun's mounting with a flash of sparks, trying to intimidate the Japanese soldiers psychologically as much as actually kill them. That was one of the greatest attributes of the Sniper, and the United States military was slowly becoming aware of the psychological and fearsome presence an adept sharpshooter could wield over the war zone, much like the introduction of machine guns had done in the First World War. By demoralizing the enemy with terror, the Sniper was becoming a nightmare ingrained into the psyche of all who witnessed the lethal effects of a sharpshooter in battle. The M1 ejected the spent casing and self loaded another bullet from the 8 round en bloc, utilizing a gas powered operating system composed of a diverted gas cylinder that powered a long piston attached to an operating rod which in turn engaged the rotating bolt inside the receiver. I scrutinized the loophole with an unblinking eye, watching as apprehensive soldiers just out of sight debated who would be the next sacrifice.

As I wondered if my superior marksmanship and tactics would keep them off the lethal weapon, a chalky, dust covered Hetai with scrapes, bruises, and cuts all over his body rushed forward into view and started blazing rounds from the Type 92 heavy machinegun. I knew these desperate Imperial Army soldiers were emboldened with the pride of their Empire and would gladly accept an honorable death in combat for the glory of the homeland and in the name of their Emperor. So I obliged him and planted a ball cartridge right between his eyes with a muzzle velocity of 2,800 feet per second that instantaneously ended the brave soldier's life. However the HMG still blasted off streams of lead momentarily as the body of the soldier slumped over the hot weapon. His nervous system had continued holding the trigger as it still had yet to realize the body was dead, although after a few more seconds it had accepted the fact and fallen away from the weapon.

A few moments later our Marines had closed the gap and began storming over the leveled barricade, spraying rounds from their Thompsons and BARs into the first set of trenches. Others valiantly raced towards the still standing southern pillbox, intent on finishing the last of the eastern bunkers. One of the first men to arrive was shot dead through another loophole by a Type 96 light machinegun before he could round the blast wall of the bunker, where the collapsed side was open to attack. The next Marine who arrived at the bunker stumbled up the loose sandbags and concrete fragments holding a M1A1 Flamethrower with a 70 pound system of three cylinder tanks strapped to his back. The first two tanks held Napalm infused gasoline and the smaller tank between the other two was full of the Nitrogen propellant. The courageous man climbed up the rubble while small arms rounds skimmed just over his head, then as he reached the blast wall he took cover behind the barricade while shoving his Flamethrower around the corner so that only the long thin pipe protruded past the concrete, where it ended in a small, hydrogen lit flame under the nozzle. The valiant Marine turned open the pressure valve at the end of his Flamethrower where the feeding hose met the gun, and unleashed a fury like nothing I had ever before seen. A hundred and twenty foot wrathful stream of flaming, thick, sticky Napalm blazed into the pillbox creating a literal firestorm inside the fortification. From out the mechanical incendiary device a fiery torrent scorched everything as a deadly concoction of pressurized chemicals surged, bouncing and gushing off the inner walls and filling every square foot of the bunker with an inferno from the ground to the ceiling. The blazing fire poured out of the loopholes and air vents, it exploded and whipped out from the collapsed wall with the thickest of black smoke billowing from every crack and crevice. The soldier behind the hellish instrument held the trigger for seven full seconds all the while flooding the bunker full of enemy soldiers with a satanic lake of fire.

Eventually the Marine curbed the flow from his M1A1 and the inhuman screams were finally heard, followed by Japanese soldiers running from the entrance covered from head to foot in the adhesive chemicals, the viscous Napalm ate through their clothes and gear while it bubbled their skin viciously in an all too slow and torturous death. Five men in total were able to exit the pillbox as the walls and floor were still burning, they ran in different directions with some being put out of their misery by .45 caliber projectiles when they got to close to newly arriving soldiers, and others left to roll futilely on the earth, clawing at their boiling skin as it peeled and melted from all over their bodies. The Napalm burned and burned, nothing could stop it, nothing could put it out until all of the chemical was eaten away by the flames, and this left the grotesque corpses of charred and melting human flesh on the steps of Piti, with the foul stench stuck in all the combatants' nostrils.

Our opening lines had fought their way past the wall and first few trenches that surrounded the village and the rest of the Marines followed their brothers inside the compound. The IJA Garrison seemed to have abandoned the eastern trench system and fallen back to the huts, houses, and seaside bunkers further inside the village. I found no more IJA from behind my scope on the interior side of the coastal base, leading Cerberus and I to jog to the damaged wall through the quagmire of the rice paddies and enter into the fray of urban combat. Once behind the wall of sandbags we jumped over the first trench in a full on sprint, and crossed the second wider trench on a makeshift plank bridge. Having already cleared the eastern trenches, we were now fighting street to street towards the sea. Another hail of Mortar rounds from the M2 teams flew over head to land on the coastal side of Piti, and maybe with some luck they'd knock out the Piti Guns as well.

Light Machinegun fire sounded off on every street, the Japanese hid in alley ways and behind huts, popping out to let off a couple shots and then diving back behind cover before we could respond. As our Marines pushed up the streets, the Hetai would throw open windows and suprise us with well played flanking fire from within the houses, hitting us in the streets hard and often. To try and deter these attacks, we started tossing MK2 Pineapple grenades into every house with an open door or window, blowing out entire walls with the concussion blast and making the enemy think twice about occupying the homes for shelter. The fighting was getting bloodier and harder the further into the town we made it, and the IJA were only getting nastier with every house we took. Suddenly a door flew open from a hut in which a furious IJA machine gunner blew apart four Marines that had been shooting down the street, his Type 99 LMG with its top fed 30 round clip knocking down man after man from their flank. Then as he ran dry on ammunition, the crazed IJA infantryman plunged the bayonet fixed at the end of his weapon ruthlessly into a fifth Marine, mortally gouging his intestines with the blade before one of our guys finally took down the Hetai with a blast of .45 ACP rounds from his Thompson.

A squad of men on the northern side of Piti discharged their BAR rifles into the adjacent huts with abandon, shredding dense paths of holes clean through the bamboo structures and still the IJA didn't budge. They may have been ambushed on the interior side of the town, but they had consolidated and reorganized into a formidable force within the village itself. Cerberus and I tried to stay low as we worked our way down the street in the central part of town with a Platoon when the canine blocked my path and swiveled his head towards the roofs on our right. It was too late as I yelled to the men in front of me to take cover, an ambush of Hetai caught most of them in their tracks with a mixture of Type 100 SMG's and Arisaka Carbines from the thatched roof tops. The six men in front of us were pummeled with bullets and I barely dove behind the corner with my Doberman leaping past me just as 8 mm rounds filled the street and sank into the hut shielding us.

More shots ripped up Marines a street over from us as I watched several soldiers drag back two wounded men gushing blood to a position behind a car. The Japanese were shooting out of every window and alley way it seemed with the last-ditch efforts of a lunatic, emptying entire clips and screaming wildly as they flanked us from behind huts or blasted us from rooftops. The chaos was on another level, it was anarchy and if we didn't change up our approach than it was possible the Japanese would repel our attack from the village. I fell back and regrouped with another Platoon and shouted at a middle aged man holding a Flamethrower, 'You there, 25 yards up this street, on the right side, there is a group of IJA on the roof hitting us hard, take out the entire house!' The man nodded and a few soldiers accompanied him as they worked up the rural village street and aimed the unforgiving weapon. I told several of the men holding a radio backpack and Comm equipment, 'Get ahold of Lieutenant Slater, and tell him to get all these M1A1 Flamethrower operators together, and assign a squad with each one to escort them, and burn down any of these huts that give us trouble, all of them if need be.'

No sooner did the group of Radio Communication Marines agree than was our conversation interrupted by a loud metallic clang, followed by one of the men in our circle falling to the dirt road with glazed over eyes. I could see his green helmet had a distinct hole punctured through it, right in line with the man's temple. In shock, one of the men screamed, 'Sniper!' We all rushed back in different directions, as I crawled behind a white marble fountain with Cerberus on my hip. The pandemonium was almost too much in Piti, with our forces just as desperate to take the town as the Japanese were to hold it. With all the shooting and explosions around us, I had no idea where we had been sniped from, and as I looked around the marble fountain, all I could see were the Marines I had just sent in down the block, with the Flamethrower wreaking utter carnage on all that stood in the way of its rivers of fire. The squad of IJA Rifleman had jumped from the roof as they were enveloped in the lethal flames, the thick Napalm blistering and scalding their faces and hands as they shrieked in agony, the smell of sizzling tissue making some of the nearby Marines dry heave. The Flamethrower operator not only set aflame the structure I had ordered him to incinerate, but the neighboring houses had also been swathed in the wicked Napalm. I thought just as well, if all of Piti had to burn in the aftermath for us to take the town, then so be it. More hidden Japanese soldiers burst out of the huts that our M1A1 Flamethrower soaked in liquefied fire, the soldiers running and rolling as they begged in agony for death. One man made it as far up the street as the fountain I used for cover, all the while wailing and scraping at the thick Napalm in futility as the cruel flames bit at his body, scorching him to the core as I watched the soldier finally collapse not far from me. The poor man's loud screams turned to a quiet whimper as his face began to melt from his skull, until he went quiet. The foul stench made me want to vomit as I looked away.

I tried to cover my nose while I continued to frantically peer around the fountain in search of the hidden assassin. I could see or hear nothing in all the mayhem, but I knew he was somewhere in this section of town, so I looked to Cerberus for any clues. His eyes pivoted from house to house, his nose smelling all the atrocities of war in every sniff. Then he paused, and stared far down the street. I peeked just over the edge and noticed a line of houses and commerce buildings, then I saw a small flash of a muzzle blast at a Fish Market window several blocks away, exactly what I was searching for. I scanned the market building, it was approximately 180, maybe 200 yards away, towards the coastal edge of the village. It was larger than most of the homes, and I scoured it from my M73 reticle for a few minutes as the battle raged around us, but I couldn't get a good angle of the storefront from my angle behind the decorative fountain.

I made up my mind and told Cerberus, 'Stay here boy, stay... Good boy.' And from behind the marble, I dashed towards the middle of the street into the kill zone of the Sniper, half expecting a bullet to pierce my helmet as I did so. At full speed I dove flat to the dirt road behind a smoking Japanes Army Jeep and crawled underneath the vehicle, dragging my Garand with me and leaving my helmet where it fell when I hit the ground. From under the axles of my new cover in the middle of the street, I took aim once again behind my M73 scope and focused in on the Fish Market blocks away. Inbetween my deadly enemy and I, the streets were filled with jetting streams of gushing flames and the lethal burst of machine guns tearing into bodies and houses. Each Sniper was in an obsessive trance, who would find who first, who would land that fatal shot on the other, just searching and destroying like cold blooded machines. There was a minute flicker of light higher up on the Fish Market, and there I found the source as I viewed another muzzle flash a minute later from a second story window as the IJA Sniper claimed his latest victim. I swiftly rotated the elevation knob two clicks, knowing each click altered the bullet strike by an inch per hundred yards. The expert Japanese marksman was behind an 7.7 x 58 mm Arisaka Type 99 bolt action Sniper Rifle, alternating his shooting from two small windows in the upper story of the log building. As our men worked their way forward behind the brutal M1A1 Flamethrower assault on the village, I tracked him to the second window but just before I could place the crosshairs on the specialist, he struck the nearest Flamethrower operator in the large fuel source tank he backpacked with him feeding his weapon, leading it to almost instantly detonate in a massive globe of imploding Napalm that wiped out the operator and the other Marines nearby in disturbing fashion. The Sniper had disappeared from the window, vanishing before I could get a fix on him as he continued wreaking havoc on all the high level targets that fell into his scope's visual. Yet as he appeared back in the first window and took aim at another American, I leveled my Garand on him within half a second and squeezed the trigger without hesitation, my shot echoing in my ears from under the vehicle. I watched as the sharpshooter dropped his Arisaka rifle out the window as his body stiffened until he tumbled backwards with a deep gouge in his face just under his hairline.

I let out a deep sigh after taking out perhaps the most dangerous enemy IJA in Piti, and relaxed under the slowly burning IJA Army Jeep, watching as our riflemen and machine gunners covered the Flamethrower operators while they steadily and methodically torched the streets house by house, either burning the Japanese soldiers alive in jets of surging fire or forcing them into a full retreat to the sea bunkers. I crawled out from under the vehicle and rushed back to the fountain where Cerberus waited faithfully, looking overjoyed to see my safe return. The battle had turned drastically in our favor with the devastating razing of the town via our infantry incendiary weapons. I witnessed nearly half the huts in Piti ablaze with a Napalm concoction induced wildfire spreading from building to building almost with a mind of its own now. Our M1A1 Flamethrowers were barely unleashing their 120 foot rivers of flames on the buildings any more, content to just letting the small house fires converge, the flames crawling across the thatched roofs from building to building. The Flamethrowers left no corner untouched by the blaze, as it travelled towards the sea while spilling into the streets and onto all the structures and huts of the crowded village until forming into a single inferno that quickly wiped out the western side of Piti with devastating efficiency. The fires and Flamethrowers uprooted the trenches on the coastal side of the village and forced the surviving IJA to evacuate their post and bunkers or risk being burned alive by the overwhelming force of it all. After another hour or so of soaking the town and western trench system with every gallon of Napalm we had at our disposal, more than half the village was consumed in the firestorm, burning down to the ground, nothing but a pile of glowing embers and ash. The last of the IJA had either succumb to the blaze or retreated into the rice paddies and jungle surrounding the village. There were bodies littering the streets, some of the corpses had nothing left to them but black charred skeletons with the the majority of muscle, skin, and fat tissues melted from the bones in a bubbling and blistering mess.

With the IJA withdrawal, the atmosphere finally calmed to a point where we could safely regroup and try to contact our main forces with the good news of our victory. The battle was a success even if it had left so many Marines wounded or worse, yet we pushed on through everything this war threw at us and were still ready for more.

Our men discovered two of the mammoth Piti guns in tact, and the third one had either been struck by our Motar bombardment or was sabotaged with explosives by the Japanese before they gave up the coastal town. The morale of our men was higher than ever as we secured the invaluable coastal guns and the rest of the village, awaiting reinforcements and our next set of orders. I sat down with Cerberus on the stone steps of a small church made of clay bricks, it would seem this was the only building of western Piti to survive the wrath of our Flamethrowers. How thankful I felt for the urban warfare to be over with, for now at least. It was too sloppy for my liking, and how lucky it was that there had been no civilians in the town before the combat had broken out. Piti was a singed pile of ashes, black smoke billowed through the streets leaving soldiers to choke on the foul odors. This style of warfare was too barbarous and miserable, our troops were bleeding out in every street and bodies littered the rice paddies all the way to the coast. It's not that we weren't ready to take the battle anywhere we had to fight, not if that is what it took to liberate Guam. It may have been inhumane to a large extent, but we did what we had to do, although Cerberus and I much preferred the solitude of the forest as opposed to kicking in doors in a congested and hotly contested city. I took a sip from my canteen as the sweat poured off my brow in the heat of the smoldering village, and we just took in the desolation as the fires still burned.

Chapter 6

The Japanese controlled village of Piti had fallen just in time, as the supremely powerful coastal defense guns were nearly on the verge of being fully operational. Cerberus and I were assigned the task of searching out any remaining Japanese soldiers that could be hiding somewhere in the compound of huts, cabanas, and pill boxes. My tireless Doberman sniffed out two IJA members hiding in a small hut on the north eastern side of town and the hut had to be grenaded as the fools refused to surrender, and then another straggler infantryman in the southern bunker on the coastline who did surrender upon being revealed. Otherwise the Japanese fortress that had been Piti was free of all enemies with the entire IJA Garrison in a full retreat from the area. Our Rifle Company was ordered to hold the village or what was left of it, until a Battalion and Armor support could arrive. These opening days of battle had been slow and traumatic, full of sacrifice by both sides as the invasion swept on into the depths of Guam herself. The earth was saturated in blood, and the Japanese were beyond ruthless, more than ready and prepared to take the war to new extremes. Nevertheless, our beach heads were expanding with the conquest of the island underway even against the more determined efforts of the IJA as they refused to surrender. After an extensive sweep of the smoldering ruins of Piti, it was nightfall and my Sergeant gave Cerberus and I a chance to catch up on some much needed rest in one of the huts on the eastern side of the town.

Inside the small shack was an uncomfortable bed, gear, multiple military cots, and clothing that had belonged to the IJA infantrymen who had previously used the lodging. In the corner there was a pot full of water and giant African land Snails still simmering, some troops must have been boiling up dinner right before we had ambushed them and raided the village. There were multiple light brown shells with yellow stripes scattered beside the pot, the shells alone were each the size of an adult fist. The Japanese had introduced the invasive molluscs to Guam so that they could dine on one of their favorite delicacies regularly. Although I was hungry, I tried not to think of food and while Cerberus smelled at the empty shells, I took off my cumbersome gear and weapons and jumped on the old bed as it creaked. I was fully asleep before my head hit the pillow, with Cerberus at the end of my bed, constantly watching over me. My dreams were replayed in my unconscious mind in an ever looping format, the radiant glow of incinerating Napalm plaguing my thoughts, and the flames hissing in my ears, only to be drowned out by the torturous screams of young men. Finally I awoke in a cold sweat to the rays of light shining through the crevices in the bamboo walls, the morning sun sparing me from the dark thoughts that tormented my inner-cognizance. My Doberman was already awake and staring at me, and without warning nosed me in the cheek and licked my face in excitement. We got up quietly while the other soldiers slumbered on the cots and made our way out of the hut to find the barracks of Sergeant Slater. The smoke still drifted across the town from the rubble and ash of western Piti, and with my dog and I feeling restless in the confines of the war torn village, it's safe to say we were ready to get the hell out of here. I found Slater in a small cabin that had been devoted to hulking radio equipment for communications, he grunted, 'Good morning Corporal, up bright and early I see.'

'Always ready to do some fighting for the Core, Sir.' I countered, 'What do you got for me Lieutenant?'

First Lieutenant Slater gave me a brief, dry smile and said, 'Hope you got some rest, they're attaching you to a new Platoon, they need a scout to lead them up some hills to Tanjo Mountain and capture a ridge that we haven't been able to take for the last few days... We can't get the Shermans up the rock face, to steep and they got all the bottlenecks on lock. Heard the IJA tore our boys up something fierce there yesterday. And.. They got a Sniper, or more probable a sniper team on the bluffs, making everything difficult. Real dangerous mission.'

I replied, 'Sounds like a grind, can't wait to get started.'

Slater waited a moment to relieve me while he reached for a smoke, then said, 'Corporal, I want to say what your dog and you did for us... Well I just want to thank you is all. That battle hinged on you getting us to the gates undetected, and there is no way them Japs thought an entire Rifle Company got behind their defenses in the jungle. You made the ambush, hell, the whole raid possible, so thank you.'

I said, 'Don't thank us Sir. Thank the men that died yesterday so that we could take Piti, those are the heros of the battle. The rest of us just do our duty.' With that I saluted and turned out the door, and within half an hour I was on my way out of Piti with a new twenty three man Platoon from the freshly arrived reinforcements. I was introduced to the Platoon leader an he explained the terrain and ridge that our Marines were getting pinned down from. The Japanese Army was evolving as the war went on, and they were learning new ways to assault and defend, much like the kamikaze attacks inwhich the desperate pilots of the Japanese Navy would plunge their Kawasaki Ki-48 light bombers into a suicidal nose dive towards US Navy Battleships and Aircraft Carriers in hopes of crashing into the great vessels and killing as many Americans as they could take with them. Likewise their Army counterparts were learning to utilize irregular warfare against our regular forces as well as a rising prevalence of attacking our lines at night. With our superior firepower and numbers, the invasion was persisting and coping well enough thus far as we made gains into the island, however the terrain was changing. The low lands that our M4 Tanks and vast numbers had been able to storm were now giving way to an ever increasing elevation where the tropical hills, rocky ridges, and mountainous jungles began to dominate the landscape. This made using armor escorts much more difficult, as the IJA had dug into the hills and mountains and were bogging our Marines down with hails of artillery and mortars, as well as sniper and machinegun fire. There would be no easy gains from here on, the Japanese had fallen back to the higher grounds in the rainforest and intended to die fighting before they gave that up.

This mountainous region benefited the guerrilla warfare and irregular tactics that the IJA had grown well accustomed to, and they were quite deadly in this theater. This only made the War Dog Platoon all that much more valuable to our Marines on the front lines, and every war dog on Guam would faithfully serve the call to battle for their country. As it were, Cerberus was leading us east of Piti and deep into the hills, and further into the lush tropical forest that covered them. I was the highest ranking member in my Platoon making me the defacto leader, not that any ranking soldier wouldn't have followed my directions out here in the bush. It was becoming obvious with the influx of Privates and the lack of Officers and Sergeants that we were spreading ourselves thin as our lines expanded across the Pacific. We marched through the fields of rice paddies as the mud caked our legs and boots while the sky turned overcast. One of the men in my squad hurried to catch up with me and the Doberman who seemed thoroughly enjoying cooling off in the murky waters, playfully bounding from one paddy to the next in puppy like exuberant leaps. I recognized the kid from one of the transport ships that had taken us across the endless Pacific ocean. The enlistee's name was Gonzales, a Private First Class from California, and one of the youths who had been swept up in the propaganda of saving the world. He said, 'Corporal, how are you?' While slapping me on the back with a wide smile. 'Haven't seen you since we got off the SS Illustrious back in the Philippines, how have you been Sir?'

I responded with a smirk, 'I've been better, that's for sure. Good to see you Gonzales, didn't think you'd make it out to Guam.'

The young Marine said, 'Yea me either, we were headed for Bougainville and at the last moment we got shipped here instead. Made landfall yesterday, I'm just ready to get into the shit.'

I glanced back at Gonzales and said, 'I'm afraid that is exactly where we are headed, right into the shit.'

'So is it true that we are going to take Smoky Ridge?' He inquired.

'We are headed towards Mount Tenjo to take a high ridge that overlooks most of the smaller hills to the west, I didn't know they had a name for it.' I answered back.

Gonzales just as enthusiastic as ever replied, 'Yea that's what the survivors were calling it back at HQ, cuz it's always foggy as hell up there and the Nips hide it in like phantoms. At least that's what I heard through the grapevine shortly after we landed.'

I muttered, 'Is that so?'

'Yes Sir.' He replied as his left boot got suctioned into some deep mud, nearly losing all his balance before recovering some what as he fell. While he had clumsily slipped to a knee before stopping his fall with his hand sinking into the marshy fields of rice, he blurted. 'And you know what else I heard. Word is that the Ghost himself is up there on that ridge...'

Another Private had double timed his way up the line to meet with Gonzales and I at the point, 'Hey, is this the guy with the Doberman you were telling me about Gonzales?'

Gonzales looked annoyed, but introduced his comrade, 'Corporal this is Richard, we call him Richy Rich cuz his father owns some factories in Detroit... Yea Richy, this is the War Dog Scout I told you about, and that's his dog Cerberus, he outranks the both of us.'

The two of them let out some jubilant laughter before Richy said, 'Wow it's an honor Sir, I heard stories about your sniper missions in the Banana Wars.'

I continued looking ahead as the two Privates followed close, 'Nothing really to be proud of there, just protecting United States trade interest in Central America. We weren't much more than muscle men for big business.'

Richy didn't lose a beat as he went on, 'Well Gonzales told me all about your dog and how you two work together as Advanced Recon, that's amazing Sir. And there is already stories spreading around the Navy and Marines that the War Dogs are here and kicking ass.'

Then Gonzales continued, 'I can't believe I'm getting the chance to work with you and your dog Sir, if what you told me is true, then we are in some good hands Richy, or paws I guess.' At that I couldn't help but join in on the laughter before I got serious again and told the two of them to drop back in line and have their guards up.

We entered the dense forest with flocks of Mariana Doves and Guam Kingfishers squawking above in the tree crowns with giant ferns and Palm trees encompassing us. Cerberus and I were on point as always, with the Platoon following, parting the thick undergrowth with our hands and swinging blades. The Strangling Fig vines of the massive Banyan trees' prop roots smothered and crushed the other forest trees and tangled every branch and bush into a spiderweb of vegetation, wrapping around boots or catching our arms. The Banyan trees grew a thick mesh of aerial roots which sprouted into a constricting grove so thick that we could hardly see through it, nevermind traverse it. I sliced my way past what I could, trying to catch up to Cerberus who parted bushes with his nose and trotted under overhanging brush and vines with swift ease. He wove between the spikey trunks of Coconut Palms and Tangan Tangan thickets like a stalking panther, and much like that top of the food chain predator, a sight of the beast would probably be the last thing many would ever see in the jungle. We sank into giant, cloudy, green puddles where the mangroves creeped up from the uneven wet soil with their complex root systems, only able to guess how deep we would sink into the filthy waters each time we ventured into one of the stagnant pools. Fungus and Mushrooms grew from every nook, and moss patches and ferns dotted the wetlands. The squad waded through the swamps, sometimes to our waist, with the brown waters sloshing around us as we held our weapons high over our heads, away from the collection of green algae aimlessly floating around the cesspools of bacteria and tadpoles. In some instances the marsh was deep enough for Cerberus to have to swim with his paws churning up the murky waters in his awkward doggy paddle. Tree frogs chirped and croaked in the background, stuck to tree trunks that rose out from the swamps as insects swarmed our faces. On the rare patches of drier land, we encountered more aggregations of huge Banyan trees that blocked the path, their large, grey, crooked trunks wrapping their host trees in crushing plant life, and forming walls of intertwined branches of Banyan figs and slithering hardwood vines.

The environment was like an oven, steaming us in the sweltering humidity as we worked our way through the tropical swamps. Then from above, the skies opened as rain pelted the canopy in sheets, working its way down the leaves and trees until soaking us from head to toe. I knew we had been lucky in the opening days, it was the rainy season here in Guam and we had avoided such a climate thus far, until now. There were roars of thunder shaking the forest and flashes of lightning through the crevices of the treetops, and I knew this rain storm wasn't going anywhere. Eventually the quagmire of tropical swamps gave way to higher ground as the forest climbed up the small hills infront of the Platoon. Ifit trees grew close together and the thousands of shiny leaflets from the many branches swayed in the slight breeze as the winds picked up. The rain kept coming down, drenching us and everything else while making the conditions miserable, the plight of the infantry was never pretty though. I paused the march, allowing the men a short break when we found some cover under the fronds of some Banana Palms and Soursop broadleaf evergreen trees. The monsoon was on us now, the sky dark and brooding, the shower steadily picking up intensity. I looked up at the clusters of the green bananas, still not ripe, yet the Soursop most definitely was ready. I knocked down one of the dark green fruits from a branch with the barrel of my rifle, and set about cutting it open and pealing back the spiked skin as I bit into the white inner flesh. The juices from the citrus were flavorful, something of a combination between strawberry and pineapple. I wiped the delectable juice from my chin and took another bite from the succulent flesh of the Soursop, and pointed them out to the rest of the Platoon to help themselves from the fruits of the forest. I knew the rain was only going to make our mission that much tougher, so soon after I decided to get back on the march so we could get to the ridge that was giving our Marines so much strife as soon as posible.

As we hiked through the undergrowth of brush and vines, I hacked away with my blade and kicked aside bushes and saplings with growing frustration. The further we moved into the young forest, the more dense it became. The downpour slowed our movements, my rucksack became saturated along with my uniform and added a couple more pounds of weight to the strain of the march. Each branch and frond that we came in contact with splashed our faces and bodies with a small pool of the collecting precipitation and all the while it continued to rhythmically beat against our helmets. Groves of Coconut Palms sprouted from the climbing hillside, the trees tied together by a complex of slithering vines that climbed and wrapped everything like green tentacles exploring from the rich soil. We fought through the knots of plant life with knives and bayonets, while Cerberus led on through the foliage while sniffing the air for scents, his thick black coat was drenched and matted and his paws were covered in mud, spiked and barbed seeds clung all over his fur like velcro. He led us higher up the hills, without the slightest care towards the torrential showers from the sky or the newly forming streams that carved into the mucky hillside as they flowed down the inclines with growing force. I was only ten feet behind the Doberman as his claws dug into the muck and mire while our men slipped and fell on the slick forest floor far behind us.

I knelt for a second to let the men catch up and signaled for Cerberus to hold his patrol, with the obedient canine sitting and waiting. That's when I noticed the movement in my peripheral vision on the tree next to me. I turned my head and squinted, just able to make out the form of a Chameleon in the leaves, slowly climbing up a Ifit branch. The bizarre reptilian creature moved in steady composure, a freakish master of camouflage without evolutionary equal. Each eye shifted independently through pinpoint pupils in search of prey or predators, its tongue which was used as a projectile tool to catch insects was twice the length of its body, and the tail of the small lizard wrapped around a twig like a fifth limb while the feet which were specially adapted to arboreal locomotion, gripped at another branch. The Chameleon moved as one with nature, confident and experienced movements always made with a purpose. It was a marvel to regard, the skin turned from a mixture of dark and light browns to a bright green overlay with dots of darker greens dispersed down its back, the skin tones changing scale by scale at command, its new cryptic coloration blending the animal seamlessly into the young tree.

I looked back down the hill at my struggling Platoon with growing concern, the young draftees had been rushed through minimal training and the overeager enlistees, well they just made me nervous to say the least. We were about to stumble into perhaps the most hostile domain on the planet, and the IJA were looking for vengeance, salivating for any opportunity they could exploit. Any single wrong movement could get us all killed. If we don't blend in with the environment and adapt, than the Hetai will pick us apart, chew us up and then spit us out as they had done to many previous Platoons that had ventured this way. And here I was taking a bunch of babyfaced boys fresh from the States up a jungle ridge to try and drive out the menacing Japanese guerillas, veterans that had caused havoc in this sector and completely halted the invasion. It made my stomach churn some while I still impatiently waited for the men to climb the mudslide, shaking my head as they slipped or grabbed tree roots and branches to pull themselves up the incline.

After the Platoon had caught up with us, I again signaled Cerberus to get back to work, trying to locate the hidden enemy that could be around every corner. One of the Officers that arrived in Piti with the Battalion reinforcements had updated me on this mission, explaining the particular ridge that the Japanese had utilized to halt the Marines from moving any further into Guam. It was a steep hill capped with a overhanging ridge that had much higher ground than any of the terrain in the west from which our forces had tried to attack from. Time and again the Japanese had utilized a combination of explosive Mortar munitions, small artillery blast, and expert long range marksmen that had resulted in heavy losses for our advances, to the point where our men had been put in a full retreat for their lives. Our superiors were going mad over this development, absolutely furious at the reports of at most a few squads of IJA guerillas were able to hold the ridge and were decimating forces of hundreds of men. The Generals felt it wasn't a good look for morale, and the Officers thought it was bad for their safety, so they assigned an advanced reconnaissance search and destroy mission to one of the new War Dog Scout Units and a Platoon of boys, no pressure I thought to myself as I parted an overhang of thorny tropical brush and forged ahead as the thorns scraped against my helmet and ripped at my hands. I decided before we even left Piti that there was two ways to go in order to take this ridge, and that was north or south of it because coming from the west was an obvious deathwish for any American. The squads jumped over deluges of rushing water that carved into the hills resembling raging rivers of muck as the storm surged on with the neverending rain draining off the mountainside, the flash flood threatening to drag us all down the hills and back into the swamps. We persisted on against the flow, pulling and pushing eachother up the ledges and steeper slopes as a team. I had taken a southern route, and allowed Cerberus to lead us on the course of least resistance. That time had seemed to have come to an end as we traversed north and onto the jagged rocks that transformed the hill into the stony cliffs and plateau that made up Smoky Ridge.

My plan of advance and Cerberus' otherworldly ability to navigate the battlefield had gotten us closer to the IJA held bluff than any other Americans could, but now my war dog was indicating the presence of Hetai at around 200 yards north of our position, on the summit of the long, narrow, ridge. The Doberman was on the trail now and I resigned myself to merely watching his movements, gaining all the knowledge of our circumstances through his actions alone. Rain bounced off his ears and nose as he smelled from side to side, arcing his snout through the wet air trying to home in on his dangerous prey with his sophisticated senses. He pointed us towards the top of the cliffs which were around a 180 yards north with perhaps a 50 foot elevation over us, maybe slightly more. As the Platoon followed the war dog, the plant life transitioned from a weave of dense jungle to a more dispersed tropical forest with a mixture of broad leaved Ifit trees and Pine conifers, mostly Ironwood. Though this made our movements less strenuous than in the thicker flora, it would only make it that much harder to close the gap for an ambush while maintaining our cover. We wove around the thick Ironwood Pines and Ifit trees that dotted the ridge, their roots digging in to the rocky terrain and cracking open the rocky terrain. Abruptly, as the ridge narrowed to a 100 foot wide sheer, Cerberus froze like a statue making me raise my M1 Garand as I peered around the mountain forest, eyeing the thickets of Cycads suspiciously while their crowns of stiff evergreen leaves danced in the storm. A few steps later,Cerberus wouldn't look up from the ground a couple yards in front of him, his signal that he perceived something unnatural directly ahead of us.

I looked to the ground and could see nothing more than pinecones and twigs, but if my dog discerned an oddity, then there was no doubt to that. The Dobie's shrewd nose could smell something, and I felt like I knew what it could be. I placed my rifle around to my back on its shoulder strap and got down into a prone position with my buck knife in hand and began to cautiously crawl towards where Cerberus stared. It was a narrow corridor formed of large protruding boulders, these structures constricted our paths and became more prevalent the higher we climbed. I ever so gently poked the soft and oversaturated ground with the tip of the blade, and then crawled another half of foot to repeat the process again and again. Minutes later, I placed the tip of the large, serrated knife into the pine needles, decaying leaves, and then into the dirt with the slightest of pressure until the tip came into contact with metal, buried only centimeters under me. It was an Anti-Personnel mine, a deceitful and lethal bomb meant to cover the Japs' rear and warn them of any approaching squads. I pulled my knife back from the earth and slowly slid backwards, away from the sensitive and vile landmine while holding my breath. Then I drew a line in the dirt and motioned for the men to avoid the area of the this sinister trap, a device that would take the legs right out from underneath anyone unfortunate enough to step on one and set off the variable activation pressure fuze. I stroked Cerberus roughly and praised him for saving our lives from the well placed Type 93 circular mine that could possibly have additional explosives buried underneath the main charge, which for the Japanese had become an extra lethal and common practice in the last few years.

Their faces looked anxious now as they followed us further up the ridge towards the well prepared Japanese force, closing in five or ten yards at a time behind the valiant Doberman. The IJA weren't far from us now, and they still hadn't picked up on our presence which is what our lives hinged on at this point. Our forces were similar in size according to the intelligence reports, but they still had the high ground and therefore the stronger defensive positions, even after all our efforts of covertly climbing in the torrential downpour. This was vital ground for the Japanese Army to hold, because all the advantages of our medium tanks and numbers of infantry and supplies were meaningless up here on the high cliffs of the ridge where mother nature allowed for but a few hardened men to claim supremacy over the battleground. We could theoretically use heavy artillery and shell the ever living shit out of the slender mountain they called Smoky Ridge due to the sea air condensing into a thick blanket of fog towards the summit, but that could take days or even weeks to successfully dislodge the stubborn enemy. The higher ups had gone with their gut and sent a new War Dog unit to scout the ridge and test just how valuable these Dobermans really were to the cause.

The IJA may have been entrenched in the higher ground, but I truly believed that the abilities of Cerberus served us as the ultimate tactical advantage in this type of warfare. The capacity to ambush the ambusher was a skill so special that it could not be measured, the guerillas may have been concealed in the forest and misty rain, but our trained war dogs were the great equalizer in irregular combat. We crouched low, right behind the prowling Doberman, the rain slowed some but wouldn't stop, and the ridge was as misty as its reputation. A minute later Cerberus gave the intimation of the hidden Hetai lines, gesturing towards the plateau a 100 yards north of our position. His body stood perfectly still giving indication of his sureness, his ears pointed forward and his eyes pierced the forest as a clear warning to me that he had found our adversary. He pointed towards an outcrop of rocks, Ifit trees, and Ironwood pines, leading me to scan the area with my binoculars to little success with the rain beating against the lenses and the mist shrouding the outlines of the mountain top in a blur. It was essential that we were the ones to make first contact, so I crouched down in a recess of rocks and gathered the troops to formulate the plan of attack and split them into two squads, Alpha and Provide. It was now or never.

I demonstrated to Bravo squad the whereabouts of the IJA and sent them on a flanking run, hoping they could sneak up the ledges and cliffs on the east side of the ridge with a superior field of fire, while I led the Alpha squad north and would engage the enemy head on, in hopes of drawing them out and allowing the second team to hit them on their three and six. That way we could encompass them from two sides at once and hopefully dislodge the IJA with enfilade fire and force them down the north side of the mountain. I put our HMGs on the Bravo squad as well as most of the Light Machineguns with the idea that those men could do more damage at closer range while I brought the riflemen with me to engage the IJA at long range. It was a huge gamble I knew, for if the second squad got caught up against resistance or ran off course, we would be in a head on firefight with less than half our strength of men and weaponry. I took Alpha squad in a stealthy, low, crouched walk with Cerberus clearing the way up to a defilade, a formation in the cliff where the rocks jutted up from the forest floor as natural barriers for my squad to take cover. We ducked down behind trees and in the recesses while we laid flat in the collecting pools of rain water, taking our time to make as little noise as possible while we set up. Cerberus settled in right near my feet, laying down in the clear, cool, pool and looking to me unwaveringly. I wanted to give our B squad the time they would need to climb the ledges on the backside of the ridge and get on location, but not too much time so that they weren't sitting right next to their combatants just waiting to be discovered and trapped against the eastern cliffs.

I ordered half of my squad to move to my right through silent hand signals and take cover behind the Pines and Cycad shrubs to spread out the line of fire. Then I had Richy on my left, ready the M7 rifle grenade launcher as he loaded up a special high powered bulletless round into his M1 Garand and with jittery hands he fixed the M7 device over the end of the barrel, securing it to the bayonet lug. Two other Privates did the same on our right, as they prepared to launch the opening volley at the entrenched IJA. The second squad of Machine Gunners knew that the Grenades would be the signal to storm from the flank and begin the assault. The men looked to me for the go ahead, aiming their modified rifles with their Grenade attachments towards the highest cliffs of the foggy ridge. My line was composed of mostly M1 Garands and M1 Carbines with only a single BAR LMG to assist us. From prone positions on the rocky earth, the men aimed down their rifles, looking for any sign of movement or trouble. The fog was vexing my Riflemen, target acquisition was nearly impossible in all the rain and fog of the mountain. Gonzales was on my left and whispered, 'Can you see anything Corporal? I got nothing?'

While I trained my rifle on the jagged ridge dotted with Pines and Ifit, I murmured, 'Calm down, look for the muzzle flashes...' I stared down the M73 scope and zeroed in on an IJA artillery man crouching behind his 7cm Mountain Gun on a steep ledge. The short barreled artillery piece on its wheeled chassis had a blast shield that blocked most of my view, except the tip of his head. The blast shield was covered in small Ifit branches that had been tied to the dull steel to break the outline of the rugged mountain weapon, but that nor the fog could keep me from finding the Gunner and another assistant nearby. I decided it was time, and nodded to Richy on my right to fire his weapon and commence the engagement. He raised up the Rifle with the M7 attachment and fired, the blank .30-06 Springfield M3 grenade cartridge exploded with tremendous recoil and the expanding gases generated propelled the MK2 Grenade forward from the Rifle as the fragmentation Grenade was heaved towards the embankments of hidden Japanese soldiers. Nearly two ounces of TNT collided against a small tree initiating the impact fuze to detonate in a powerful blast of black smoke, splintering the tree as it tumbled down to the wet sod while the detonation hurled jagged, searing, metal chunks in every direction. From the other Grenadiers, more shots rang out across our line as concussion explosions blasted apart small trees and rocks, sending the jagged, broken iron bouncing off the rough ledges and into the crevices of the cliffs where it fortuitously impaled a few of the unseen Hatai.

Before the artillery gunners could turn their hulking piece towards us, I let off the first shot, dropping the gunner and knocking off his dark green helmet with a well placed ballistic to the dome. While our three Grenadiers reloaded their M7s to launch another volley of Grenades, I focused the crosshairs on the assistant who had dove behind the Mountain Gun after watching his comrade hit the dirt. Then I found just a sliver of him appear through the wagon wheel spokes and under the axle, I placed the cross hairs and squeezed the trigger and after the rifle jolted, I checked to make sure the soldier was taken out. I could see his face through the rusted spokes of the old artillery piece, from there it was apparent he was neutralized, with a massive gouge in his right eye where the .30-06 had excavated his entire orbital socket into a dark hole that spilled burgundy onto the cliffs. The startled Japanese soldiers began to shoot back in a panicked induced reaction, showing their dismay as they lost composure and shot randomly into the forest below them. The guerilla force couldn't believe it was they who had been bushwhacked, and in their own domain no less. With the erratic sprays of rifles and machineguns lighting up the misty darkness and giving away their positions, the rest of our rifles started shooting back from behind stone protrusions and thick trees. My eleven man squad was holding its own, and from behind iron sights our marksmen were picking off the distressed IJA as they were absolutely stunned in the opening sequence of combat.

We kept searching out the flashes from the barrels of our furious enemy and listening for the angle of gunshots from those still coy enough to remain concealed. Eventually though the Hetai were able to get their bearings and started tearing up our location with a Heavy Machinegun, striking one of my men in the gut directly through a tree trunk. Our Grenadiers launched a second round of the fragmentation Grenades at the ledges and overhangs with earth shaking explosions sending shrapnel filled infantrymen flying off the cliffs. The guerillas were fearless in the face of our surprise attack and had already reorganized their infantry lines behind new cover and began laying down heavy suppressive fire in our direction. I began to wonder where the fuck our second squad was as we started to receive the full frontal assault of the Japanese warriors. That's when it went from bad to worse, as I saw one of our boys run from a bullet riddled Ifit tree in an all out sprint until he dove behind a Pine. Only in midair as he dove, I watched the Marine's head burst open as his brain matter scattered in bloody chunks out the side of his forehead from a devastating exit wound. Before the kid hit the ground next to the tree, his life had already evaporated from his body. A look of fear was rapidly plastered on many of the young Private's faces as one screamed, 'Sniper!! Get down!'

Before I could look back from the last fatality, another Marine was already laced in the head where he had laid, firing his Garand into the enemy lines just seconds prior. This time I could hear a distinctive high pitched crack of a rifle blast, leading me to realize there was a Japanese Sniper raining terror down on us with a Arisaka 6.5 x 50 mm Type 97 bolt action rifle, probably equipped with a 4x scope just left of the receiver and a five round clip. Judging by his incredible marksmanship and choice of weapon, it was apparent this guy was a professional. His skill and fieldcraft were masterful, and his knowledge was expert as he used the smaller caliber 6.5 mm Arisaka, for its high pitched cracking noise and small muzzle flash after firing made it extremely difficult to locate, especially in a battle of this tenacity. Meanwhile a Type 3 HMG Taisho 14 was pinning us down from a hidden machinegun nest and made just trying to get a shot off next to impossible.

I risked a look from behind an Ironwood Conifer and scanned the rocky ledges before I planted my scope cross on the chest of a semi concealed Hetai in some thickets of young Screwpines, blasting off 7.7 mm Arisaka rounds from his Type 4 Japanese Garand. Without warning a maniacal Hetai jumped out of a nearby spider hole and ran towards our left flank with a Type 100 Submachine Gun, slinging 8 mm bullets in the ground all around us as mud went flying in the air. Just as he turned the corner of our rock embankment and into our exposed left flank, I discharged my M1 towards my last mark, thinking that if I was going to die, I mine as well make sure I take one last bastard with me. I rolled over to my back as the Garand ejected a shell casing and tried to swing my rifle on the intruder that had broken our lines as he shredded one of our Marines with a quarter clip of 8 mm Nambu bursting at 450 rounds per minute. He already had his SMG fixed on me in his chaotic rampage when Cerberus charged from behind me in a blur of shiny, soaked, black fur, his carved muscle rippling down his entire body. The irate Doberman was halfway to the soldier in a single bound and caused the man to pull his aim from me and direct it at the rapidly encroaching nightmarish beast. The Hetai pulled the trigger in an automatic burst as Cerberus leapt into the air where he was struck in the ribs just as he crashed into the soldier and knocked him off balance and to the ground. The canine was completely oblivious to being shot and regained his stance on top of the soldier and pounced, clamping onto his arm with the ferocity of a wild animal until an audible crunching sound indicated a crushing break to the ulna bone in his left forearm. Blood flowed from around Cerberus' mouth while the desperate man screamed and struggled to get away from the clenching jaws as the dog snarled and wrenched him about. With the mighty canine mauling and overpowering the Hetai, he desperately reached for his Type 100 SMG to try and finish the job. Cerberus was in a full on bloodlust and released the Japanese man's arm only to instantly sink his fierce, sickle fangs deep into the man's neck as blood gushed while he savagely shook with pure intensity, his jagged teeth carving deep into the jugular and trachea. I watched in awe as my dog, perhaps my best friend even, continued to clash with the soldier as they were caught in a life and death struggle, thunder and lightning shaking the sky.

For the first time in all my experiences, I was in shock as I witnessed the mayhem unfold in the downpour, the soldier grasped at his weapon in the mud just out of his reach while punching futilely at the chaotic canine. Cerberus shook the man's head back and forth through a demonic growl, with blood spewing everywhere, oblivious to all else until Gonzales from a short range away blasted the man's chest with his Garand, officially ending the soldier's agony at the hands of the wounded and wild animal. I rolled down the rocks and crawled in a pool of water over to Cerberus as quickly as I could while still under heavy fire to check on him, grateful to only see a single bullet had hit him. And although it had left a deep laceration that bled profusely down his side, under further inspection I was sure it was only a flesh wound. I yelled for Cerberus to lay back down and nodded over to Gonzales with grave appreciation, before crawling back behind the nearest Ifit tree to once again take aim. I could here the 'pings' of Garands running out of ammunition and the roar of Grenades detonating, with Richy just missing the newly found HMG nest high on the ledges with a frag Grenade from his M7 launcher as he let out a sigh followed by a string of expletives. I scanned the battle in vain for the Sniper, trying to notice any setting that looked too contrived or just something out of place, but I found nothing. Instead I settled my rifle on a LMG wielding infantryman who knelt behind a thicket of brush to slap in a new clip, but before he could cock it back to chamber a round I had already delivered a .30-06 Springfield that sliced through his neck from one side to out the other, nearly taking off his head like a scythe. I was beyond pissed, just thinking about my dog being shot by these brazen guerillas, and I was looking for vengeance every time my finger found the trigger.

Our lone Browning Automatic Rifleman was unloading a slew of .30-06 Springfield rounds when he peaked just a little too far around a Benguet Pine tree and collapsed to the ground clutching his chest from a well placed Arisaka round. I couldn't believe it, there was no way to get a read on him, I yelled, 'Shit, this sharp shooter is killin' us!'

Gonzales responded, 'Yea I heard over the radio transmissions on the transport ships that the Ghost was here on this ridge!'

With bullets hammering the rocks in front of us, I barked, 'Who the hell is this Ghost, Gonzales?'

'Hiroo Kozuka!' He answered in between gunshots, 'The legendary Japanese Sniper, they claim he killed hundreds in the Second Sino-Japanese War! You must have heard of him...'

'Yea, I heard of Kozuka, so he's the Sniper that claims Smoky Ridge, huh? We will have to see about that.'

We were taking some of the most accurate long range rifle fire I had ever seen and we were bogged down by a brutal HMG nest on top of it all. Richy had reloaded another Grenade and raised up to a crouch, steadying his sights on the Taisho 14 HMG which blazed with 6.5 mm Arisaka so hot that the barrel fumed in the rain like a smokestack. Just as he steadied his modified rifle, his shoulders slumped and his head dropped as he fell back to his knees and we heard the high pitched crack echo off the cliffs and boulders. I grimaced already knowing the outcome, there was a rush of blood from under Richy's heart where he was hit, and before he could fall flat, another shot viciously nailed him in the head. His limp body collapsed as Gonzales cried out, 'Richhy! No, no, Richy, hold on!'

I jumped on Gonzales and yanked him by the elbow hard to the ground as he still reached for his fallen buddy with another Sniper round whizzing just over our heads as the bullet hissed through the rain. I bellowed, 'He's gone man, Richy is gone! Do him a favor and keep your fucking head down, that's all you can do now.' I knew if Gonzales had made it to Richy's body, he would have been the next victim of Kozuka, that notorious Japanese Sniper was playing games with us, turning this encounter into a bloodbath.

Gonzales was still in a irrational fervor, the pain displayed on his tormented face as he tried to pull his arm free from my grip and rush over to his friend. 'I have to check on him, I have to see if he's still alive!' He yelped pitifully.

I dropped my Garand and slammed the distraught Marine to the muddy ground with both hands, and yelled in his face as I shook him, 'It's too god damn late Private, he's dead! If you want to do something about it, then pick up your rifle and start shootin' back, that's a order son!' I let go of Gonzales and picked my M1 back up and crawled forward behind some bush cover and Pines to try and get a grip on a losing battle. I could feel the bile rise from the pit of my stomach, this mission was not going to plan and it was looking like we could end up trapped up here and slaughtered, we were outgunned and they held the higher ground to compound the disaster.

It would seem that I had come into a head to head conflict with a Sniper whose abilities could be too much for me to handle. I don't think I had ever seen a better marksman than myself, but this Kozuka was doing things I had never seen and with such confidence, it was quite intimidating to be caught out in the open with a Ghost that I couldn't even find. I hollered to the remnants of my squad, 'Where in the fuck is Bravo?' Their faces were all wrenched in a torn panic as the Japs bullets churned up the forest and earth all around us. I could feel the IJA formation methodically slithering up our flank with their Sniper pinning us down unmercifully. Our Medic was ducking behind a small boulder as enemy fire sparked off the sides, he was desperately trying to pinch of a hemorrhaging artery in the leg of our last Grenadier as he clung to life.

I looked back to Cerberus who ignored the gunshot wound on his side even as blood mixed with the rain drops and dripped off his ribs and chest. The heavy machine gun seemed to have stalled, momentarily giving us a reprieve from the overwhelming spraying as the Taisho 14 HMG crew changed out the overheated barrel for a fresh one. Just then a tree exploded right behind us as it caught the wrath of a 7 cm Artillery shell from a new Mountain Gun that had been wheeled over to bombard our position. The deciduous tree came toppling down behind us as wooden splinters and shards of steel fell all around from a shock wave that shook our brains. I prayed that this wasn't the end for us, my men's lives depended on me, yet I was watching them drop left and right, one after another. I realized that Cerberus depended on me too, and then it clicked that the only way I was going to get us out of here was to lean on Cerberus and all of his potential.

The Mountain Gun smashed another tree behind us, this time cleaving a tall Pine in half, and as branches came crashing down all around us, I yelled for one of my last five soldiers still standing to throw a smoke Grenade and try to conceal our position for a few minutes. The fog and rain was making everything difficult, but these adept IJA infantrymen were able to find us and pin us down through the mist just fine. It was time we changed that, and as one of the canisters landed about twenty feet from our location, thick smoke fumed out. A few more of the smoke Grenades were thrown until the cloud was nearly a hundred feet wide as it swirled in the winds and blocked off our enemies' view of us. I told my Marines to find new spots before the smoke cleared, and I got behind Cerberus as the unstoppable an unshakable dog galloped into the grey smoke as I followed right on his heels. The Doberman could not be conquered and seeing that alone had raised my spirits enough to take the fight to them. Blood coursed out of his ribcage with every heartbeat, yet the prideful Dobe paid no heed to his injury, almost like he couldn't be bothered with it. Cerberus' muscles flexed down his back legs and the rain was shaken from his fur with every athletic leap he took towards his mortal foes, his ears moving and keying in on every noise behind the dense smoke tendrils. As it began to clear, we found ourselves in a grove of Umbrella Pines and located a fallen tree, we swiftly dove into the hollow in the ground formed by the upturned roots as they draped over us. I told Cerberus to lay down in the back of this alcove and pulled globs of the mud from all around me and covered myself, my arms, my face, and my hair with the wet dirt and clay. Then I laid down with just the white of my eyes and the M1 barrel poking out from our new nest, and I searched the ridge for prey. I glared down my M73 scope, and scanned everywhere, under rocks, in bushes, in patches of grass, in caves, I searched not like I was hungry, but rather as if I was starving. My ravenous eyes finally zoomed in on a tall Ironwood where I thought out the corner of my vision I may have seen a muzzle flash though it could have only been some heat lightning from the storm.

As I scanned up the tree behind my scope, I became aware to the probability that my men and I more than likely were not going to make it off Smoky Ridge alive. I kept studying the tree and then I heard shots from the east, there was a sound of machine guns ringing in my ears, and it sounded like a lot of them. I glanced over my optic from out of the root system and seen my second squad had finally showed up to the party. Bravo unleashed their automatics with ferocity on the IJA, flooding them from their exposed flank with singeing lead blasting in every direction. Heavy Browning M1919s swiveled on their tripods over the new front, but mainly concentrated on the Type 3 Taisho 14 HMG nest tucked back in a rocky crevice of the cliffs, peppering it with a thousand rounds until the HMG was disfigured and its Gunner team was a pile of bullet riddled flesh. BARs unloaded in burst after burst from behind the IJA and for the second time in this battle these Hetai were ambushed, most of them turning too late to avoid being chopped down by our Marine's savage fury. They pushed on and stormed right through the IJA lines that had been concentrating their full attention on our first squad Alpha, who had been bogged down to the south. Machinegun crossfire raked the IJA infantry to pieces, the heavy weapons cutting into their formation's side until it started sending some of the men backpedaling. The IJA lines withdrew soldier by soldier away from this new onslaught, they were outmaneuvered and their will to hold the ridge slowly waned in the face of this second assault on their flank.

I kept scanning the tree with no suggestion of the Ghost anywhere to be found, and I wondered if my mind was playing tricks on me. That's when I saw it, the flash came from the tree adjacent to the the one I had my scope trained on. One of our Browning M1919 Gunners had been struck in the head followed by the high pitched snap of the Type 97 Arisaka, and less than a second later his Assistant Gunner was also laying face down in the mud, lifeless. The discreet holes in the soldiers' heads were undoubtedly the Ghost's calling card, and I was about to lay eyes on him and see if I could put the famed Kozuka in my sights for a change. I pressed the butt of my rifle hard against my shoulder and swung the M1 towards the tree, scouring the Pine through the scope while my free hand adjusted the elevation dial a few clicks as I scrutinized every branch on the tree that overlooked the entire ridge, this tall Ironwood serving as the Ghost's pedestal over the conflict zone. His camouflage must have been phenomenal because the more I swept my scope up and down the Pine, the more I felt he wasn't in this tree at all. The mist circulated over the craggy mountain top, wrapping around the rock formations and trees, concealing so much as the rain fell over the battle. Our B squad pressed on with the perforated barrels churning out belts of ammo and hacking the IJA soldiers to bits while their positions were overrun by our Marine comrades from the east as they successfully infiltrated the guerillas' flank. Our spate of attacks had reduced the Japanese hold over the ridge, and the mounting bloodshed was taking its toll on both sides now.

The gun battle still waged all over the summit as the Snipers remained engrossed in the hunt, trying to single handedly turn the tide of the struggle all around us. I scanned up the tree again and my eyes caught the slightest movement of a bending branch. I placed my reticle on the pine needle covered limb and barely made out the definition of a soldier who appeared more plant than man. The Sniper's helmet was wrapped in a net that held small coniferous twigs and branches, and his face painted dark brown and grey was almost entirely obscured by eerie, dark, weeds that dangled from under his helmet over his neck and down to the marksman's shoulderblades. The Pine branches enshrouded most of his uniform which was tattered brown and green cloth with more offshoots of slender branches and pinecones secured to his body as he hugged tightly to a large branch high in the tree. Even his 6.5 mm Arisaka had small twigs tied to it, arcing out in multiple angles like that of a natural branch and the barrel had been painted a dull mahogany as he directed his precision killing tool from his forest throne. I clicked the elevation knob one more degree and steadied my own precision instrument with the sole intention of proving the Ghost wasn't the immortal nightmare that all seemed to believe. As the crosshairs slid over the man's center, my heart jumped from my chest as he suddenly altered his rifle at a downward angle, staring directly at me with unearthly, empty, eyes. In that spine-chilling moment where the world and all its chaos stood still, we simultaneously pulled the triggers of our Sniper rifles as the explosion of gunpowder seemed to shatter time itself.

The mud imploded right in front of my face as I rolled rearwards to the bottom of the pit and on top of Cerberus. I couldn't believe he missed his shot, regardless if it was by inches, I was too fortunate just to have my head intact. Cerberus looked at me as if he was annoyed that I was laying on the poor wounded dog, but I sure as hell didn't want either of us to catch one of those Sniper rounds. After a few minutes passed, the gunfire seemed to have quieted down, so I took off my helmet and crawled to the root covered entrance where I slowly raised the helmet far away from me with an extended arm. When it wasn't shot right out from my hand, I raised it further from the hollow of uptorn roots and still no Sniper rounds took the bait. I carefully crawled up and surveyed the tree and checked where the Ghost had been. He was gone. Had I slain him I wondered as I got out and told Cerberus he could follow as we investigated the aftermath of the deadly clash. Bravo squad had taken the summit with rifle support from the survivors of our Alpha squad, and the IJA had been forced to withdraw down the northern slopes of Smoky Ridge. The rain still drizzled over us as the men began making sweeps of the fissures in the cliff ledges. After finding no more pockets of IJA on the summit, the Marines rejoiced that we had somehow taken victory from the clutches of defeat, and claimed the dreaded ridge for Uncle Sam and America.

Cerberus and I made our way over to the tall Ironwood that had been Kozuka's sniper nest, and searched for a body on the ground, only there was none. Then as I looked up the tree, I found the unmistakable hue of blood, spread across a few of the branches from someone on their climb down. Cerberus sniffed at more splotches of the blood as they were diluted on the forest floor by the rain, the heroic war dog still oblivious that he himself was leaking blood from his ribs. I was astonished at the Doberman's bravery, ready and willing to sacrifice himself to save my life as he dove teeth first at a ruthless IJA soldier bent on murder, and undoubtedly prevented a massacre on our flank. Around his muzzle, there were still traces of blood that had yet to be washed out by the rain. As he stared with an intensity into the forest, I stroked the wet Doberman's back and looked around the summit of the ridge with awakened ambition. A new resolve emboldened my spirit, that this Ghost bleeds was all that I needed to know.

Chapter 7

Upon a meticulous sweep of the area, my Marines were confident that we had ousted the Imperial Army from Smoky Ridge. I had ordered the Platoon to take post on the perimeter to prevent any counter attacks and to gather our dead and wounded. Then I had Private Murphy use his radio backpack to try and raise contact with our Companies just west of the hill who were hunkered down in the swamps and awaiting our signal to start marching up the western face. Now that my force had succeeded on the clandestine mission and deposed of the IJA threat, it seemed prudent to get reinforcements up here to the strategic ridge, less we let it fall back into enemy hands yet again. I found a small lean-to shelter made of thin logs and yellow palm leaves thatched into a roof. It was dug in and out of the rain so I had Cerberus wait there while I found our Medic to see if he could take a look at the dog to clean his wound and patch him up.

The Medic's name was Private Smithers, he seemed intimidated and was a little jumpy to be poking around the gunshot wound of an agitated Doberman Pinscher. He said, 'Goood boy, good boy. Easy now... It's okay, just got to take a look at ya.' I held Cerberus' head to my chest and tried to calm him down while the Medic used a set of surgical forceps and a Iodine swab to explore the wound, he pushed against the shattered nerves and torn flesh, and finally managed to get a reaction from the stoic canine as the dog yanked his head away from me to turn and inspect this new man that was prodding at his fresh injury. This caused Smithers to fall backwards on his ass with his eyes wide, expecting a snapping set of teeth coming at him at any moment. Instead the Doberman stared at him with inquisitive and wary, dark, eyes, trying to figure out who and what this Marine thought he was doing. The Medic said with a shaky voice, 'I'm sorry about that boy, just trying to get a thorough look at the wound.'

I responded for Cerberus, 'It's alright Private Smithers, just tell us how bad it is.'

Medic Smithers went back in cautiously, first with a swab of Cocaine Hydrochloride as a local anesthetic, then with the the hemostatic forceps and poked around the tender laceration getting so close his nose was nearly touching the Doberman's fur. While he continued to inspect the injury using gauze to try and pull some of the blood out of the way, another Private walked into the lean-to from out of the storm and said, 'Sir, Private Jones reporting. The ridge is completely cleared but for some small caves under one of the cliffs. What should we do about them?'

I responded with growing agitation as I pulled my attention away from my dog to answer, 'Stand guard at the entrance and I will deal with the caves when I'm ready. Where in God's name is Private Watson? And what in the fuck took your squad so long to get on their flank? You had us hung out to dry for far too long Private Jones.'

'Sir Private First Class Watson is dead, Sir. He got hit by a Sniper as soon as we had joined the fray.' The energetic Private responded, 'I apologize for the hold up Sir, we encountered a land mine field on the back of the ridge, we lost Private Gomez to one soon after the initial fire fight began.'

I mumbled, 'Son of a bitch.' Trying to count all the bodies in my head.

At that another Marine came over to the small makeshift shelter, this time it was Murphy saying, 'Sir I haven't been able to get anything but static from up here on this ridge. I can't raise the Companies for nothing, what should I do?'

Hesitating, I looked around the lean-to, regarding the maps scattered about the sod and the tea cups on a plate next to a pile of rice and chopsticks. This mission had cost my Platoon too many lives and nearly mine and my dog's as well, then I returned, 'Just keep trying Private, this storm isn't helping much, that I can tell you. Whatever you do, don't come back until you have reached them either.'

I looked back at my dog and seen Medic Smithers spraying out his bullet wound with some Iodine solution while Cerberus seemed annoyed and ready to get away from the field doctor. I spat back to Jones, 'What are you still doing here Private?' He jumped and immediately left back into the downpour and towards the caves.

As I stared into the hypnotic rain sheets falling over us, Smithers finally broke my trance and said, 'Corporal, it's just what I expected, only a flesh wound. He got a glancing blow and a bullet had cut clean through his side and glanced off a rib or two with no structural damage to the bones. His pupils and gums look good, I can find no signs of internal bleeding and it surely isn't an open chest wound cause his breathing is normal with no blood in the lungs, which is great news.'

I nodded my understanding and appreciation to the Medic, and replied, 'Thank you Smithers, that is good news.'

He answered, 'No problem Sir, we'll just put a bandaid on em. Got to get this hell hound back into the war after all.' His attempt at a joke to cut the tension and ease the worry I felt over my wounded friend showed the Medic's strong people skills, but I wasn't in the mood for it. I had seen wars take so much, from families, enemies and strangers, from towns, cities, and from entire countries, yet you really don't understand the evil implications of war until it starts taking something from you personally. Smithers pressed fresh gauze onto the wound and then began wrapping an adhesive white bandage several times all the way around the Doberman's torso and chest as tightly as he could so as to hold the gauze in place over the flesh wound. He then gave Cerberus an injection of Morphine Sulfate into his front leg just above the paw. Smithers finished his work by saying, 'He will probably be coming out of shock soon and be in a whole hell of a lot of pain as his adrenaline and such wears off, so this should help make the pain more tolerable for him through the day. If he starts acting strange or tired, he may need an IV of blood or fluids, but right now he looks healthy. You're going to want to watch that wound closely, biggest danger to him now is infection and sepsis. So if you can keep the wound clean, allow it to drain, and change the bandages regularly, I think this Doberman will make a full recovery. Good luck Sir.'

I dismissed the Medic and sent him to go check on our wounded men he had already worked on, and see if they were still stabilized. Cerberus was content to be out of the rain and I took off my jacket and wrapped it around his torso to try and keep him warm and his wound dry. I crouched down and embraced the Doberman in a solid hug that he wasn't accustomed to, still the sleek canine wagged his nubby tail and licked the side of my stubbled face as I whispered, 'You saved my life boy, I owe you so much, you don't even know.' His dark auburn eyes closed joyfully as I roughly scratched his chest which caused his back leg to kick, and this let me know the resilient war dog felt just fine. I grabbed a dish to fill up with rain and set it down for Cerberus to drink while I looked over the maps in the shelter. They were covered with lines that seemed to indicate the progression of the front, and many Japanese symbols were written on the sides, I knew the characters were their alphabet Hiragana, but I had no idea what they meant. A water droplet landed on the map as I held it in my hands, more followed suit with the thatched roof of the lean-to succumbing to the monsoon. I figured we should get back to the grind and clear the last possible pockets of resistance on the ridge, there was no rest in jungle warfare.

Just as we were getting ready to head back out into the storm, Private Murphy ran up to us and shouted, 'Sir, I still can't get a response from the Lieutenant... I don't think my radio can negotiate the atmospheric interference of the storm.'

'Yea that, or these Japs are jamming the radio channels Murphy.' I said perturbed. 'I thought I told you I didn't want to hear any more god damn bad news. Now get our wounded and fallen Marines all under this lean-to as quickly as you can, and see if you can help out our Medic with anything he needs assistance with.'

We made our way to the cave entrances through the slop of the soggy ground, rain bouncing off us as I scanned the top of the cliffs which were strewn with rubble and warped pieces of what looked like Radar dishes. With Cerberus wrapped in my green coat with the sleeves tied together under his abdomen, we found a limestone ledge overhang forming a large void in the cliffs and a shelter from the rain within the ridge itself. Private Jones was posted inside it with two other Marines, all staring down their weapons that were nervously pointed towards the two dark caves in the back of this chasm. There was several cots and tents inside the access, with some fancy Radar computers and hulking radio equipment covered in a canvas tent with generators nearby. This must have been a Radar Installation at one point, at least until our Bombers or Battleships bombarded it to scrap metal. I checked the tent and recognized a Type 94-3A Radio with its powerful transmitter and a hand cranked generator. I knew that could definitely get a signal off the mountain, monsoon or not.

The Marines looked relieved when I showed up with my war dog, and backed up some as I allowed Cerberus to approach the end of the chamber which led to the mouths of the caves to see if he could perceive even the faintest odor of humans wafting from within the rocky abyss. The cavern seemed to be naturally carved out by the rains of eons past, the wounded Doberman smelled the first entrance on the left and gave me no sign of an enemy presence in that side, so he walked closer to the second access and raised his snout to test the air. His triangular ears went high and pointed forward and I knew he detected IJA in this entrance. I ordered Jones and a comrade to check the left chamber for supplies and anything useful and to allow me to borrow one of their Thompsons for my own cave exploration. Next I ordered the remaining Marine to go find Murphy and have him utilize the much more powerful Type 94-3A Japanese radio and see if he could get any transmissions out to our Companies. I regarded the entrances into the cliff side, the left one was short and it required the soldiers to crawl on all fours just to get inside the tight cave, while the right one was much larger although barely shoulder width at many points.

I sat my M1 Garand up against the rocks and since we were under the limestone ledge that provided cover from the elements, I also removed my rucksack. Cerberus had somehow managed to take off the coat that has been wrapped around him, exposing his bandages but I realized the jacket bothered him so I just attached the tether to his collar and prepared for the descent. We entered into the chasm where the light was slowly choked out from existence and our vision became obscured with debilitating darkness. There were unlit torches at varying intervals along the way, but to illuminate my path with one would be like holding a neon target on my chest for the IJA to shoot at from the cover of the insidious shadows. With one arm I held the Thompson at my hip while following only a step behind the Doberman as he sniffed out the IJA in pure darkness. I may have been a trained Sniper, but I was more than proficient with any Light Machinegun, and I had even been at the reigns of a few HMGs as well. Damn near blind, I simply followed the leash of Cerberus as he steadily pulled me forward, he was dazed some from the drugs that the Medic had given him, and yet his abilities were as sharp as ever as he smelled into the far reaches of the fissures and inhaled the scent of the cunning Hetai, a volatile enemy that still refused to give up the last defenses of the ridge. There was a cooler, stale air current flowing through the cavern, a musty smell emanated from the floor, and there was green moss growing on the walls but it quickly dissipated into stone as we hit total darkness around the first corner. I was on edge in the silence, my eyes betrayed me as I raised my weapon around every boulder, swearing I was looking at the silhouette of a killer.

I ejected the magazine and checked the 30 round box clip of the M1 Thompson to make sure it was full before slapping it back into the sturdy Submachine gun. We proceeded around the next bend as I held tight on Cerberus' leash while he pulled me around the corner of the winding crevasse, his nostrils inhaling and his ears turning and zoning in on the most miniscule sounds in a range far higher than any human could dream of hearing. My eyes were steadily becoming more adept in the cavern, yet without the Doberman I mine as well have been blind. I nearly stumbled to the ground as I tripped over a jutting rock only to step over a drop off two steps later, causing me to fall to the stone floor with a racket as the Submachine gun crashed to my side. I picked myself up and brushed off the Thompson, furious at my clumsiness in the gloom of the cavernous pit. Cerberus waited for me to regain my composure before tugging me forward as I carefully placed each foot down softly, searching for the limestone floor. Stalagmites began to appear, the sharp structures growing out of the ground about knee high, as if I needed anymore dangerous tripping hazards. We descended over ten feet down a steep slope, the Doberman's claws scraping the stone as I gripped the rough ceiling to slow my momentum, then as the tunnel leveled into even ground once again, I could see a faint glow a ways ahead.

The narrow conduit began to widen as we entered a huge chamber and the solid ground was covered with a sticky film, the whole place held a dank smell to it with a hint of ammonia. As I strained my eyes towards the top of this expansive chamber, I could see the ceiling itself was moving, swaying and twitching. Cerberus' head leaned to the side, then to the other side as he listened intently and watched the movement with his glowing eyes. Unexpectedly, something dropped from the stalactites and swooshed down nearly grazing my head before unfolding massive wings and rebounding in midair as the megabat glided past us and with a few flaps of its enormous wings it was gone, deeper into the cave. I looked back up to the mass of stalactites, the stone icicles formed from calcium salt residue left by dripping water, and within this matrix hung hundreds of Guam fruit bats. The giant old world bats were sometimes called Flying Foxes due to their dog like faces and ears which closely resembled Cerberus', they had brown fur flecked with grey over most of their bodies and golden patches on their mantle and necks. They chirped and squeaked at the disturbance we were causing as Cerberus' ears went crazy trying to pick up all the sounds, their wings wrapped them like miniature sleeping demons while they stared down at us from their roost. We continued on from under the colony of megabats as the fresh guano stuck to my boots in stringy, fermenting, clumps while I checked for any other foot prints in the excrement.

We ventured closer to the glow of the torch as the flames flickered and cast light dancing against the walls. A stream seeped from out of fractures in the cave and filled up the indentations as it cut into the stone, filling the tunnel to our ankles while it flowed deeper into the lair. We came to the end of this extensive chamber down to a split in the cave, with a passage way going left and the main one continuing on straight, with the shallow running stream following both routes in the diverging fork. Now I was wishing that I had brought some backup if just to clear the other borrow, instead I had my Doberman check with his perseptive nostrils inhaling the mixture of molecules floating in the air, savoring every hint of our enemy moving surreptitiously in the blackness. The hell hound's three hundred million olfactory receptors were absorbing the atmosphere with each breath through his long snout. The canine's nose was capable of detecting odors in the parts per trillion, an ability to smell so inconceivable and sophisticated that humans struggle to comprehend it. Each respiratory cycle circulated more odors to the olfactory receptors, trapping them in a labyrinth of turbinates that filter the odor-laden air near where a massive section of the dog's brain was dedicated, receiving electrical signals from each receptor for processing. The Doberman was even able to decipher which nostril the scent was coming from, and exhaled out of the slits on the side of his big wet nose so as not to disturb the constant introduction of more odors to the front of his nostrils. Cerberus was locked in and he could taste the enemy in the abyss, there was no hiding from the beast.

He pointed towards the small lair on the left and craned his long neck towards it with his horned ears stiff, his muzzle pulled back revealing his razor-edged incisors and jagged, bone crunching molars as he growled. I stepped towards this entrance with my feet splashing in the subterranean stream and wrapped the tether around my forearm twice as the incensed Doberman dragged me into the new pit. This crevasse became confined as the walls closed in on my sides, squeezing against slick rocks that scraped against my ribs and chest, crouching under oversized stalactites and stepping around the protruding stalagmites that rose from beneath, all while the burrow grew dimmer as the torch light dissipated the further we explored. The corridor grew so tight that we were forced to crawl in a few of the bottlenecks, the darkness was overwhelming and I could only pray we didn't get stuck in the mountain's natural dungeons. Eventually he made our way around some smooth boulders and I could stand again, finding the restricted cavern open up some as water dripped from above. I could see a glimmer from a torch begin to cast a twilight on the cavern from a ways ahead when Cerberus abruptly halted making me run into him in the murkiness. He stared at the corner, unmoving, telling me without words there was danger behind it, waiting.

I unraveled the leash and gripped the Thompson in both hands, stepped in front of the Doberman and hugged close to the cool stone wall, then I jolted around the corner ready to unload the clip when I heard the hissing and stopped dead in my tracks. Something flashed at my head in a blur. I only avoided it by dropping backwards to the wet floor on my back as the serpent struck again in another flash of shadows, snapping its venomous fangs at me once more. Cerberus took a step towards the deadly and irreconcilable Pit Viper before I caught him with a hand on his chest and pushed the Doberman back. I crawled backwards a few paces still laying on the ground as the enraged Viper lashed out again from high above us. It was only then that I could see the tail of the greenish snake was tied in a knot around a root that slithered out from a crack in the ceiling of the cave. The damn snake nearly bit my face with its terrible fangs teeming with haemotoxin venom whose enzymes caused irreversible necrotising of the flesh. The IJA had set a crafty trap, placing the pissed off serpent around a bend, stuck hanging from the ceiling by its tail and trying to get ahold of anything that moved. I signaled to Cerberus to crawl and we wriggled underneath the Pit Viper as carefully as we could, not getting to our feet until we were well clear of it.

We were back on the trail in the desolate depths as water trickled down the smooth walls of the limestone and dropped on us from the stalactites overhead. The light was gradually permeating the endless cave when my Doberman declared the presence of a foe just ahead. I demanded with a silent hand gesture that the wounded dog wrapped in blood stained bandages should stay here, and with a scornful look from his glowering eyes, the dog turned his head from me and laid down gingerly. Cerberus had done his job, and done enough for one day, I wouldn't risk his life when I was sure I could handle the Hetai by myself. Holding the woodgrain foregrip of my Tommy Gun, I stalked stealthily further into the depths, the narrow cave began to open into a wide chamber with a single torch flare radiating a soft reddish glow over the darkness. There were a bunch of wooden crates stacked high against one side, a couple hammocks were on the other side with one occupied by a slumbering soldier, the hanging beds allowing troops to sleep off of the wet limestone where a few inches of water methodically drifted down the chasm. I heard whispers of Japanese behind the crates as I ducked down behind a large stalagmite before creeping up to the crates from the shadows. The whispers came to an end as my foot made a tiny splash in the water, and I heard a machinegun cock back as I blitzed from behind the boxes and let off the M1A1 Thompson, erupting with a strobe of white light while pumping the two startled soldiers full of .45 ACP full metal jackets as their bodies shuddered and shook. The stopping power of the rounds nearly lifted the suprised infantrymen off the ground as they staggered back and fell into the pools of the cave floor, turning the waters red as the blood diffused from the bodies.

I turned back to the stuck Hetai, tangled in the hammock, struggling and rolling to get out of the net of rope that had him suspended in the air. His eyes went wide as he yelled something indiscernible and the Trench Broom chopped him up in an instant, leaving him hanging only to fall face first into the stone, his right leg still caught in the hammock, awkwardly half suspended in the air and dripping blood from where he had slept just seconds earlier. Out of nowhere the wooden crate next to me was knocked violently off the stack where it had collected a slew of 8 mm Nambu rounds from a Type 100 SMG in the crevices towards the back of the chamber. The crate fell at my feet where it split open, spilling small boxes of various calibers of ammunition all over the stone floor. I hit the deck behind the other crates and clawed my way a short distance on my elbows before I regained my posture and crouched against the wall of crates. There was another burst from the shadows of the lair as the boxes splintered apart with bullets holes from left to right just over head. The shots resonated off the chamber like a deafening roar, I snuck a peak between a slit in the stacked wall, trying to find where this hidden soldier was shooting from. I got to the opposite end of the crates and pushed the last box over some so I could fit the barrel of my Thompson inbetween the gap and reciprocated the Submachine gun fire with my own. My Annihilator sprayed, sweeping the darkness with round after round at 700 per minute as cartridges were ejected and reloaded from the blowback system, the box clip feeding the devil's piano one after another.

Again the crates were strafed with return fire, the blazing Type 100 SMG shaking the wall of wooden containers behind me while bullets passed right through it with minimal resistance. I sprinted from the barrier in an erratic weave, dodging stalagmites and other stacks of crates as I ran towards the wall where I found cover behind a protruding ledge. From there I countered back and let off a burst from my Thompson at the specter in the rock fractures as .45 pistol rounds sparked and ricochetted off the cavern stone in deadly flurries. We were spraying at one another, desperate in the dark realm to land a shot from our turbulent automatic weapons without being hit in all the madness. Then the last footsoldier rushed from a crevice in the limestone, screaming the battle cry 'Tennoheika Banzai!' with his SMG slinging lines of bullets into the ledge protecting me, chipping the stone into flecks and dust. I stuck the Thompson around the barrier and blasted a succession back with a .45 ACP round finally whacking the soldier in the thigh, accompanied by a burst of tissue gouged out by the velocity of the heavy bullet. Then the Thompson clicked harmlessly as my clip went empty while the man stumbled to his knees, only to get up and yell again 'Long live the Emperor' in his foreign dialect. In shock, the wild fanatic continued his charge with the Type 100 Shiki Kikan-tanju's perforated chrome barrel lighting up the cave with a few more rounds of lead before it too clicked dry.

I came from around the stone ledge and squared up to the combatant as he stumbled forward lunging his SMG with the bayonet blade at my abdomen. I sidestepped the deadly point of the bayonet while smashing the crazed Hetai in the chin with the wooden butt of the Thompson as I heard bones crack in his jaw, and yet the rabid soldier only went more berserk in his rage and slashed at me again as I darted sideways, slicing into my arm and causing me to drop my weapon. He sprang at me with utter abandon leading with the sharpened bayonet, thrusting the blade towards my chest until I evaded the charge and leapt to the left as the manic soldier skimmed past me. Before he could turn I rushed him and seized the soldier in both arms, picking him up into the air with all my strength and carrying him two full steps before body slamming him to the earth, impaling him on a pointed stalagmite. Gravity combined with the infantyman's own inertia plummeted him onto the honed limestone structure, the stalagmite puncturing completely through the Hetai's back and ripping out through his stomach, the sharp rock was covered in the man's squirming entrails and others bits and shreds of viscera organs.

He moved for another minute or so as I kicked his SMG away from his reach and waited for the warrior to pass on from the gruesome predicament. When I looked up Cerberus was staring at me, the wounded canine unable to keep himself from trotting down the foreboding cave to investigate the sounds of struggle between his master and the sworn enemy. I greeted the dog with a huge smile as I could see his concerned eyes glimmering in the torch light, and then we inspected the countless crates of Japanese ammunition. The Doberman had not only found four IJA guerillas hidden in complete darkness, he also located a valuable ammo depot that could have supplied an entire Japanese Rifle Company for months. This was one of the main purposes the Marines invested so heavily in Doberman War Dogs, their noses, ears, build and demeanor were the precise blend necessary to create the perfect dog of war.

We explored a bit further into the chamber and at the end, we found where the water pooled and drained into a compact tunnel that no man could fit through, so we worked our way back from the lair with the ammunition depot and through the cramped quarters and confines of the caves, back towards the surface. Cerberus inhaled the damp cavern air and found no scent of any enemy, at least any enemy that was still alive. Having cleared the last pockets of the Imperial Japanese Army from within the ridge, we trekked our way to the surface, finding the light at the end of the cavernous tunnel just ahead, and exhausted when we finally made it out from the depths of darkness. There was a group of Marines stationed in the void that had previously served as the old Japanese Radar installation. Private Murphy was waiting at the entrance, saying excitedly, 'Sir, Sir I got great news... What the hell happened to your arm Sir?'

I told him, 'Nevermind that, give me a rag or something to tie around this scrape. Now tell me what the good news is Private.'

Murphy replied, 'You were right, that Type 94-3A Japanese radio was able to get my transmission out and I got ahold of the Rifle Companies. The Lieutenant said they were marching up the west side of the hill as we speak and should be here shortly after night fall.'

'That is exactly what I needed to hear Murphy, excellent work.' I retorted as I began to inspect our wounded men on the cots. The rain was still coming down in a constant drizzle, the mist rolling off the ground in thick clouds of swirling fog.

Private Jones walked over to stand beside me next to the lines of our wounded, with Medic Smithers working fervently on one after another, checking their dressings, setting up IVs, and taking pulses. Jones said, 'Nothing but a few food stores down our cave, how'd you make out Sir?'

'Four dead IJA.' I stated with a pause, 'And one hell of a ammo depot, probably a hundred thousand rounds hidden in one of the branches of that cavern. Shiki, Arisaka, Nambu, Mortor and Artillery shells, boxes and boxes. Cerberus sniffed it out without breaking a sweat.'

Private Jones blurted, 'Four IJA guerillas, and a massive ammo cache, shit.. Amazing work Sir.'

I thanked Jones for the compliment and handed him back his Thompson, before I walked to the far corner where Gonzales was standing by himself, overlooking the line of our fallen Marines. 'How you doing Private?' I said, looking down at the pale, blue, body of Richy.'

Gonzales looked up with a distraught face and answered, his chin quivering 'You should have let me accompany you and Cerberus on the cave clearing Sir.' He then looked back down to the pale form of his fallen brother.

I told him sternly, 'Take your time Gonzales, we all lose friends in war... Best to write home, maybe a letter to his mother. Try to express how Richy died heroically in battle, for freedom, and for his country. Other than that, there is nothing you can do son.'

I slapped him on the shoulder and left the somber man to mourn, letting the cold reality sink in. It was the truth, there was nothing left that he or I, or anyone for that matter could do, except carry on. War had a way of making your brain kind of short circuit on normal functions, and concentrate entirely on survival, just focusing on surviving day to day and minute to minute, like our ancient ancestors once had to. In a way it made the fighting easier, almost tolerable when the warrior was in a state of primal thinking, tapped into our instincts. Although war would never be right, in this case it truly seemed to be a necessary evil, and that was the only reason I signed back up. A minute later I found Cerberus scarfing down some rations that some of the Marines were feeding him. I called him over and he trotted to me, more like a horse than a dog, elegant even through the pain of his injury. We found a vacant cot and I fought exhaustion while I got some supplies from the medic and changed his bandages and checked the laceration. The durable Doberman panted as I administered wound care to the chiseled canine, and when

I was done, we collapsed on the cot and passed out as my thoughts tried to escape all the turmoil and bloodshed trapped in my mind, searching deep within my subconscious for refuge.

War dog checking cave for Japanese stragglers on Iwo Jima

Chapter 8

During the middle of the night, F Company had arrived at the summit and by the early morning hours G Company began rolling in. At 0600 hours I awoke and rolled off the cot to the sound of a steady drizzle outside. I exited the tent with my dog and could see the sheets of rain coming off the cliff overhang while Marines trudged in, soaked and exhausted from a hard night march through the storm. I was surprised to see two Doberman war dog units had accompanied the men and I instantly recognized the handlers of a scout unit and a messenger dog from our War Dog Platoon. I tried to stifle a yawn as the Messenger Unit approached us, their blue female Doberman Pinscher Pepper bounded over towards Cerberus while her floppy ears fluttered, then she lowered her front end to the ground in a playful stance. Cerberus' docked tail wagged excitedly as his triangular ears shot straight up as he greeted the dainty female. Pepper nosed Cerberus in the face and the two instantly began to dance, with Cerberus headbutting the blue girl in the side and Pepper throwing her shoulder into the black Doberman's chest, leading them to spiral in circles as they chased one another with playful bites and rough slaps. I let out a hardy laugh as the two joyfully frolicked, and although Pepper gave up easily 25 or 30 pounds to her male counterpart, she was as fierce as anything I had ever seen, slapping Cerberus with her little paws and baring her long teeth as both their nubby tails wagged sporadically. I hadn't seen my boy this happy since Camp Lejeune, and while the dogs were enthralled with one another, Pepper's handler Sergeant Dunlap asked, 'Corporal, how are you?'

'Well I'm breathing Sergeant, so I can't say that I'm doing too bad.' I replied, 'How has your campaign been thus far?'

Dunlap just shrugged his shoulders and looked to Private First Class Gallo, as he spoke up, 'We got transferred to this sector yesterday Sir, and we were stuck in the swamps and rain the whole day. Before that we had been providing support over on Fonte Plateau for the 21st Regiment, holy shit was it some bitter fighting over there. Nips were everywhere I swear, behind every palm tree and in every ditch, and some of their damn bunkers are thicker than my ol' ladies tush.'

I replied amused, 'Is that so?'

Gallo said, 'Oh yea, I'm telling ya, especially between Chonito Cliff and the Bundschu Ridge, bastards are determined not to lose any more of that sector. They're bringing in a lot of reinforcements from the north.'

Sergeant Dunlap cut back in, 'What the hell happened to your dog?' While pointing at the bloody bandages and medical tape wrapped around the canine.

'Japs grazed him with a 8 mm SMG, lucky, lucky, boy.' I stated with a thankful expression.

Dunlap replied, 'For sure he is. Best take even more precaution than usual, word is the IJA have recognized the importance of our War Dog Units and been aiming for them as valuable targets in battle. There was a couple killed in action yesterday.. Just a fare warning Corporal.'

Private Gallo glanced around the bunker and then asked in a quizzical tone, 'So where's Blanchet at?'

I looked towards the makeshift medic tent and the growing line of dead Marines on the rocks, as some of our severely wounded weren't able to make it through the night, and said solemnly, 'K.I.A... We were making a sweep of a compound we had taken, an, well.. Michael fell to a booby trap, tripped the switch.. Didn't make it past the opening day.'

Gallo didn't say a word as Dunlap nodded, and remarked, 'Sorry to hear that Corporal, he was a good soldier, and the Marine Core will miss him.'

A moment later, Private Gallo added, 'The preliminary bombing of Guam definitely wasn't the cure all. Admiral 'close in' Conolly scorched the earth for two weeks, and what do the IJA do, they just bunkered down to weather the storm and then crawled out of their caves to light us up before we even stepped foot on the beaches...'

Then the Sergeant continued, 'We've lost a lot of good men, and it looks like the Japanese are strengthening their Regiment's forward lines around the Fonte Heights, and on Mount Tenjo too. General Takashina is trying to box us in and not allow us to join the beachheads.'

I asked, 'So how's the advance going on the Orote Peninsula, Sir?'

Dunlap answered, 'Not well, we haven't even attempted a push towards the West, there's a massive mangrove swamp that's nearly impenetrable and entrenched with close to 5,000 Japanese. But Major General Bruce and General Shepherd did seal it off with the First Provisional Brigade, for now.'

I responded, 'At least there's some good news on this God forsaken island.'

Then out of nowhere, Gallo gave me a narrow eyed glance and inquired, 'Sir, there is a rumor going around the ranks that you battled the Ghost up here, is it true?

I replied, 'Uh yea, yea it is Gal..' I stared off into the distance as the nightmare of that Japanese Sniper's bullets striking my men one after another plagued my mind for a brief moment. 'The deadliest marksman I've ever come against. He killed a lot of my men up here, that son of a bitch. It didn't look good either, yet I somehow managed to hit him when we flanked the ridge, but he escaped with his Platoon down the northern slopes. Slippery as he is deadly. Still, we took the high ground from them, however, not before he inflicted a lot of damage.. I've never seen anything like him before. Bastard skimmed me more than once.'

'Holy shit that's amazing!' Private Gallo exclaimed, 'I can't believe you survived to tell us about it Corporal. He had been picking off our Officers from a thousand yards at the base of this ridge for days, had the Companies scared to shit, pure dread… You know, I heard nobody even knows how old he is. They say the Ghost was fighting for the Imperial Army back in the Great War.'

Sergeant Dunlap interjected, 'Yea and now that Kozuka survived a shot from one of our best Snipers, the new rumor will be that he's fucking bulletproof.' Dunlap and I exchanged some hearty laughter, meanwhile Gallo didn't look very amused, but eventually cracked a smile.

Our conversation was interrupted as Cerberus tackled Pepper between the three of us, only for Pepper to roll over on her back and nibble on his neck with her dagger fangs. We all chuckled at this as I said, 'Better keep an eye on these two, the last thing we need is a litter of puppies running around the Guam battlefield.'

At that I took Cerberus with me to find Major Skaggs who was in charge of both the Companies and see what our next objective would be. Smoky Ridge was covered with hundreds of Marines, some were setting up .30 cal Heavy Machineguns on the crest of the cliffs while others stacked sandbags around them. Mortar teams were putting their guns together and soldiers erected canopies against the rain and others dug into trenches and assembled outpost, scraping together logs and rocks into improvised bunkers tucked into the Pines and crevices in the ledges. Not twelve hours after taking the ridge and our men had already turned the terrain into a Marine stronghold and a bastion of liberty in the brutal mountainous jungle. A line of Carrier based light bombers flew over the slender ridge, the low drone of their engines a precursor to the payload of warheads they were about to drop. I found the Major's tent in the rear of the bunker and reported, as Skaggs exalted me with a smile and firm hand shake after I saluted him, 'Corporal, come in, come in and have a seat. Great work yesterday, and you have to tell me, how did you take the ridge?'

I answered, 'Honestly Sir, I just followed my Dobie. He brought us up the south side and then... Through much sacrifice and a fortunate maneuver or two, we shocked them and forced them off the north end.' .

Major Skaggs retorted, 'I'll be damned, that dog brought you right to their position?'

I said, 'Yes Sir, then we took a beating head on until we caught them with some automatic flanking fire, simple as that really.'

The Major replied, 'Not as simple as you say Corporal, my Foxtrot Company had been repelled from concealed locations on the South Eastern trails for two days, then we lost several Platoons in the massacres that followed when we tried to rush the Eastern sheer. Those fucking guerillas always had the edge on our advances, an exposed our weaknesses like true veterans with their hit and runs. That fucking sniper there, Kozuka, had taken control of the entire ridge.. If I had known that these Dobermans were so adept on the point and such successful scouts, I would have requested a squad of your Dog Units back on D-day.' I thanked the Commander as he went on, 'Are you sure there is no pockets of Japanese holed up in the crevices on this ridge son? No stragglers we have to worry about in the caves?'

I told him confidently, 'No Sir, I had my Platoon comb the entire ridge and I personally explored the caves myself with Cerberus. This zone is completely secure.'

Skaggs replied, 'Good, I just didn't want some band of infantrymen sneaking around behind our lines at night and sabotaging our gains. The gotdamn IJA did just that in the northern zones, got a squad past the gaps in an outposts near Adelup Point and made it all the way to the beaches where some Japanese Demolition Engineers blew up an entire ammo dump, fucking disaster if I've ever seen one... Then another squad of these bastards snuck back behind the lines in the dead of night towards the 1'st Brigades Mobile Surgical facility and attacked a few of the medical tents. Japs ambushed the guards, killed the Doctors, and shot the nurses in the back as they ran for Christ sakes. Shit, before they were done, they even bayoneted the wounded patients, and then they were off back into the night without a trace.' He paused as he thought about the desperate tactics being employed by the IJA. "Now to business, my intel reports state that there is a massive infantry buildup of the IJA and their 9th Armored Regiment has moved in tanks from the interior of the island. The IJA are consolidating their lines on Fonte to the north and right here on Mount Tenjo to the East. Same thing is happening to the South with the

1'st Brigade getting slammed from the Alifan and Lamlam mountains. General Takashina has drawn his lines in the sand, and Guam is a powder keg right now.' The Major took a moment to light a cigar as he looked out into the downpour from our rocky bunker as Marines bustled in and out around us. 'So what you did in helping us secure Smoky Ridge was essential for this sector, as this little sheer is the gateway to Tenjo Mountain. Now I just got orders from Division Headquarters that Lieutenant Putney has assigned three War Dog Units under my command, I will be reattaching your Dobermans to Golf Company under Captain Malcolm, and you'll be on the forward advance. Since we have this valuable ridge, I will leave Foxtrot Company here to form up a defensive position for our force beachhead line, and I want you to escort my other Rifle Company down through the Aguada river valley and lead the first assault on Tenjo.'

I replied, 'With just one Company Sir?'

Major Skaggs stated confidently, 'Don't worry Corporal, I'll be sending more Rifle Companies as they arrive from the beachhead to form an assault force and the Army is assembling their own strike force as well. There is a few medium tank Platoons working that way with the Army's 77th infantry in the zone just south of us. They should, be able to send some M4 Shermans over to assist us, and the higher ups want us to form up with Army when you get there. That way we can move our infantry in as we pound their position with the Shermans and some 8 inch artillery fire from our M1 and M115 pieces that their hauling. The Generals just want to make an engagement on the Mountain and maintain the push East to keep the pressure on the IJA. You'll be working with Lieutenant Mason of the 77th Infantry and my good friend Captain Malcolm to try and gain a foothold on Tenjo, at least until the rest of our Medium Tank battalion and infantry reinforcements arrive from the beaches.'

'Understood Sir.' I answered with a salute as I was dismissed by the Major.

We were to be on the warpath by 0700 so I tried to grab a meal and traded the cigarettes in my rations for some chocolate with one of the Medics. Then while I changed the bandages on Cerberus, I sent a Private away to get me some en blocs for my M1. He must have seen my frustrated expression when he came back with only a few magazines, as he told me the ammunition and fuel supplies were near a critical shortage. It wasn't exactly what I wanted to hear before heading out to one of the most fortified mountains in not only Guam, but perhaps all of war torn Southeast Asia. I finished wrapping up Cerberus' wound, placed the en blocs and hand grenades in my pack, and started getting our Company together. I would be working under Captain Malcolm, but under all intensive purposes the mission was on my shoulders, though the load would be lightened by the other Dobermans who would serve our outfit. The other Scout unit was composed of a powerful dog named Silver, the black and rust Doberman looked similar to Cerberus, only with a much shorter military crop of the ears. His handlers were First Class Privates Herkiemer and Dadian, both had done well at Lejeune back in North Carolina, and I'm sure were handling combat just fine. Meanwhile Pepper with her handlers Gallo and Dunlap would work as the Company's lone messenger unit. Before we began the descent from the mountainous sheer and into the valley, I had requested to Captain Malcolm that the survivors of my Platoon be assigned to Golf Company and he obliged, allowing me to form a squad of trusted men directly under me, including Medic Smithers, infantrymen Jones and Gonzales, and even radio specialist Murphy.

We started marching down the southern face of Smoky Ridge into the storm, our fifty pound rucksacks getting heavier with every drop of rain they absorbed. The inclines were slick and new streams merged and ran down the hillsides, winding between tree trunks and boulders, every step was precariously placed in the slick, mud laden, forest floor. The tropical conifer woods slowly gave way back to the sprawling rainforest dominated by the Coconut and Palmettos converging on every front, with Banyan trees occasionally parting the undergrowth just enough to see the dark clouds above. The winds picked up and blew the fronds of Palm trees all to the northeast, the trunks even bending some as the storm pressed the forest with mighty gales of over 40 knots. The column of over two hundred Marines followed the Scout dog units as Silver and Cerberus led the way down Smoky Ridge. Fronds and leaves blew wildly at the men as the rain pelted us from every which way, and yet the infantrymen kept marching off the ridge. Silver and his handlers stayed far on the left, while Cerberus and I took the right, our recon units clearing the dangerous forest ahead of the hundreds of Marines safely behind us. The Scout dogs patrolled nearly a hundred feet ahead of the Company, their superb ancestral sensors scanning a thousand feet further. The two black Dobermans worked in tandem as they plunged through the foliage like apex predators, acting as two tips of the forked tongue that led the serpentine body of battle hardened Marines ahead, smelling out our deadly prey. But while Silver was restrained by leash, Cerberus had the advantage of working off leash, this rare ability based on exceptional trust between him and I, which was almost unheard of in our War Dog Platoon. Meanwhile Pepper's unit wasn't far behind us, with my squad deployed as her cover team.

Our Doberman units continued on point until we eventually came to the Aguada River valley as we completed our hike off the rugged ridge and entered the second generation limestone forest, where the lumbering Ifit and Giant Monkeypod trees stifled out the undergrowth. The canopy was covered in colorful flocks of tropical birds squawking as we passed under, this new jungle terrain made for easier marching as our Doberman scout dogs brought us towards the turquoise river that cut through the center of the jungle, her tributary streams spiraling out and feeding the old forest. We marched around craters that had singed the trees around them black and curled the leaves, these war wounds in the earth left by our naval bomber runs, and found some game trails that allowed our rifle company to more easily traverse the thick vegetation. The rain slowed some as we neared the river whose level was rising quickly from the monsoon's downpour and reaching into depressions in the earth and flooding trees in a couple feet of rising water. I kept the river on my right and sent Cerberus ahead to sweep the foreground with Silver's team while always maintaining sight of the Aguada as Golf Company followed in formation behind us towards Mount Tenjo. The gully was beautiful, as Eucalyptus trees sprouted near the water's edge, the bark on their trunks peeled in strips and the vivid white flowers brought an array of beauty to the dark forest. The Monkeypod trees were also flowering as their giant crowns which spread nearly two hundred feet in diameter were dotted with pink poofs as their petals floated down on us in the rain. I followed Cerberus through the ancient forest, the twisted branches above were so tightly intertwined that light barely hit the forest floor in most spots. We jumped over massive tree roots and countless puddles and streams, the rains mercifully subsided to a light sprinkle and within seconds deerflys and mosquitoes had swarmed the entire Company, the incessant insects biting at any exposed skin around our hands and faces. The men swatted at the pestilent swarms as they tried hard to focus on the dangers that could be lying in wait, scratching at bug bites while holding weapons ready in the shady forest.

Eventually we reached a flooded transport road, and soon after we were joined by an armored Platoon with four medium M4 Sherman tanks to offer a defensive shield as much as a new offensive spear to our Rifle Company. It was a beautiful thing, the Army and Marines working together, shoulder to shoulder in the wet jungle as we pushed on to make our assault on the IJA. One of the tanks was even hauling a 36 foot long M115 8 inch Howitzer, the brutal gun with its 17 foot long barrel would undoubtedly be vital in bombarding the Mount Tenjo fortress soon enough. The four, twenty foot long, dull green, war machines crumpled brush and small trees as they rumbled through the forest, carrying fatigued Marines and with their tracks churning up the narrow, muddy, road while taking away all the stealth of our encroachment. It didn't seem to matter much, the scout dogs weren't picking up any scent of the IJA in the river valley which brought a uneasy feeling to my already shot nerves. Throughout this invasion, there hadn't been hardly a single advance by our troops that hadn't been struck by a Hetai guerilla force or two. However, I trusted in our Dobermans, and if they didn't smell the foul stench of our dangerous adversaries in the forest, then I was sure that there wasn't anything to worry about.

We continued following the river, a light drizzle keeping our Company drenched as the river kept rising, leaving the roads to resemble swamps that had us trudging through mucky water that was knee deep in many sections. The Sherman tanks kept our pace up, the Company leader Captain Malcolm was pushing the men with haste to complete his objective. A few minutes later the Company came across a small herd of Philippine deer, spooking the slender creatures back into the jungle and away from the river's edge. Not much further did we march than did Cerberus stop dead in his tracks with his ears pointed straight as arrows towards our twelve. A few moments later Silver and his handlers doubletimed over to us, with Private First Class Herkiemer exclaiming, 'We got enemies ahead, Japs maybe a couple hundred yards out, Silver is sure of it.'

I answered, 'Yea, no doubt about it, Cerberus picked up the scent of them too. Someone better inform Captain Malcolm.' Private Dadian ran to the rear tank in our column in which the Captain was hitching a ride on top of the huge M115 Howitzer being towed by the Sherman. While Captain Malcolm was busy conversing with the tank Commander who was standing half out of the tank's main turret, I pulled out my military map and studied the terrain with Herkiemer, trying to think like the enemy. The march was soon halted and the Captain approached us with a pissed off expression plastered on his face.

'Can somebody please tell me the meaning of this?' Captain Malcolm asked.

I replied, 'Sir, we have detected a enemy force ahead waiting to ambush our Marines. The dogs are a hundred percent certain of that.'

Staff Sergeant Hanchett, who was the Tank Commander and leader of the Tank Platoon that the Army's 77th sent over to assist us, made his way over. He looked gruff, grease and stubble adorned his face as he squinted at us from behind tired eyes, asking 'What do we got going on boys?'

The Captain gave a sideways glance towards Hanchett before he quipped back, in a irritated tone, 'So what?.. We got orders and a schedule Corporal, and that isn't any god damn reason to halt my advance.'

Before I could answer, Private Herkiemer stated bluntly, 'Sir, we know the orders, Sir. But the Corporal and I were looking over the tactical maps, and well.. About 200 yards East, there is a bottleneck up ahead, a bridge.'

I picked up from there, 'The dogs smell a fucking ambush, Sir. That bridge is going to be a shooting range for them Hetai guerillas, and we need to send in an advance reconnaissance squad to assess how to proceed.'

Captain Malcolm looked from me, back to Herkiemer, and then at our dogs with a scowl before saying, 'What are you soldiers suggesting? That we hold up here in the middle of the jungle while your units scout the rest of the valley?'

I answered, 'That is exactly what we are suggesting, Sir.'

Malcolm replied, 'And how long would this reconnaissance take?'

Dadian responded, 'Hard to say Sir, maybe a couple hours.. Could be more, maybe less.'

The Captain looked incredulously at our war dog units, 'I don't have time for this bull shit. I got specific orders to meet up with the 77th at the base of Tenjo by 1300 hours. If we wait for your recon, than my Company will not make the rally point with the 77th before nightfall, and I can't leave the Army out to dry on this one. We push through whatever is ahead behind our armor, these M4 Shermans should handle a guerilla force with no issues.'

Then Private First Class Dadian pleaded, 'Captain, it's a trap, you gotta listen to..'

Malcolm hissed, 'Private, if you question the chain of command again, I'll have you put in the goddamn stockade for insubordination before you finish your next word!' He glared at the three Scout Unit soldiers, then at our two dogs with the rigidity of a true Commissioned Officer, then asked with growing frustration, 'Staff Sergeant Hanchett, do you have any problem moving your tank Platoon to the point and advancing over that bridge?'

Tank Commander Hanchett answered with a queasy look, 'No Sir, no problem at all.'

Captain Malcolm stated, 'Excellent, those Hetai will probably run back to Tenjo when they see our tanks anyways. Alright now, let's get a move on to the rally point. Move out men.'

A Gunner Sergeant who had been near the back of our meeting, eagerly squelched over the Company, 'You heard the Captain.. Move out!!'

Staff Sergeant Hanchett gave us one more look of angst before turning and climbing back into his M4 Sherman. Then Dadian murmured, 'Chain of Command, huh? I get he wants to impress the Generals, but running into a Japanese noose to hang ourselves ain't gonna impress anybody.'

Private Herkiemer replied, 'If it's so important that we be there to support the 77th, than did he ever stop to think that it's better we arrive later than not at all?..'

I looked at Dadian and Herkiemer and warned them, 'You're right. Be ready for anything, I got a bad feeling about this. It's been too quiet for too long.' At that we were back into formation, but now the medium tank Platoon was at the point, and as we came around a bend in the road, it led to a straightaway towards the bridge that extended over the swelling and swiftly moving Aguada river. I knew the more rain that fell on Guam, the more valuable the bridges would become to our movements. It was common sense, the rivers were flooding from the monsoons and rushing with white water currents in many places, meaning the shallows where our troops could normally cross at were dwindling, that is, if any were left at all. This change in weather and water level made these bridges the only routes to advance and therefore far greater targets to the Imperial Army.

The column of Marines clenched their weapons in the ready position, the tension rising as we all peered around the dense jungle walls and ten foot tall river grass surrounding the mucky lane as we marched. I clicked off the safety on my M1 Garand, and hooked Cerberus' leash to his collar, all with the unmistakable feeling of being watched. The last hundred feet seemed like a mile on the water logged road in this narrow corridor between the tropical hills and rushing waters, Cerberus and Silver were going crazy, signaling to hidden Hetai all around us in the bush. It seemed like a nightmare, knowingly walking into danger while trying to warn deaf ears in vain. I was all for following orders when they followed reason, but sacrificing men wasn't a numbers game to me like it was to the Generals and Admirals. And if orders meant walking your own men into a firing squad, or gunning down innocents, well then I would never understand 'just following orders'.

But as the first M4 tank crossed the old stone bridge, there wasn't a disturbance in the natural environment, just the deep rumble of the diesel motors that rattled the cobblestone beneath its steel tracks. The next medium tank began crossing the small stone bridge and still there wasn't a shot fired. I caught a smug look from Captain Malcolm towards the rear of the Company and thought maybe we'd get lucky, that our armor and numerical advantage had intimidated the IJA and would keep them from engaging our Company as we passed on to make the rendezvous time with the 77th at the Mt. Tenjo rally point.

Boooom! Baboom! Babababooomm! The earth shook and the flooded road rippled at our feet with concussion impact tremors as the bridge detonated in a series of fiery, interconnected, explosions. Gigantic fireballs rose from under the bridge supports, swallowing the tanks within the flames. The Japanese demolition engineers had wired the structure to blow with gross amounts of TNT, and now the larger rubble was collapsing to the river with small stone debris flying and landing all around us as a mixture of grey smoke and a cloud of vaporized dust slowly enshrouded the detonation site. I could just barely make out the silhouettes of our flaming tanks falling through the rapidly disintegrating bridge, the wreckage steaming as the hot steel submerged below the rushing waters, our armored brutes sinking uselessly to the bottom of the swift Aguada river.

Shell shocked, and immediately down two of our Shermans, the forest and river grass lit up all around us with muzzle flashes as bullets ripped through our ranks, mostly on our Western flank. Our remaining Shermans began to reposition towards the new fire fight with their turrets taking aim as our men hit the ground and attempted to find any defilade possible to avoid the storm of bullets. Golf Company followed our training that they had drilled into our heads, and started laying down covering fire for one another as we searched out new positions for shelter from which we could counter attack. But that's when the IJA unleashed their secret weapon, and from one of the hilltops on the northside a 20 mm hail of High Explosive shells pummeled one of our M4 Shermans, the large HE rounds ravaged the tank with explosive impact after impact, rattling the ground beneath us. After collecting a slew of the shells that punched holes clean through the behemoth and twisted and warped the metal armor, the Sherman finally detonated into a massive, fiery implosion as one of the 20 mm HE rounds had finally struck the tank ammunition inside setting off a chain reaction. The annihilation of the M4 tank resulted in the killing of not only the five man crew, but also the small group of Marines and Army infantrymen that had been using the tank as cover, launching their flaming bodies into the river.

The muddy waters of the road were bursting in small arms automatic strafing everywhere as men screamed out in horror. The mammoth gun on the hillcrest began lowering it's angle of trajectory, concentrating on the M115 203mm towed Howitzer. The auto cannon pummeled our biggest gun to flaming wreckage, neutralizing its greatest threat in mere seconds and only continued its devastating onslaught, hitting our last Sherman with some glancing blows and leaving a path of volatile explosions in its wake as the automatic flak cannon tore through our ranks and down the road, cleaving bodies in half, ripping limbs clean off, impaling soldiers with shrapnel, and flinging our Marines like ragdolls all over the road. Gallons of blood diffused into the ankle deep water turning the road into a burgundy stream, bodies were shredded into unrecognizable lumps of singed flesh, all the while I stood staring up the hill, trying to find the brutal weapon in complete shock, my ears ringing and my vision shaking as the grotesque scene was processed in my mind.

Just when I thought the situation couldn't get any worse, a high pitched whistle droned over us, then another until the lobbed mortar shells landed in the midst of our infantry formation, launching their wrathful shrapnel in muddy explosions that impaled our soldiers by the tenfold. More whistles were heard as the Japanese garrison directed the shells at the mass of our infantry column, taking over the ambush as the auto cannon cooled it's overheated barrels, and readied itself to raze our discombobulated troops once again. A set of explosions landed just south of us, the blast deafening as the shockwaves were felt in my chest. I looked back just in time to see Silver and his handlers Dadian and Herkiemer become enveloped in the smoke and debris of the mortar blast. As the smoke cleared, I watched, stunned, as Herkiemer reached out with a bloody arm high in the air as he and Dadian were laid out flat on the road, covered in mud, tore to pieces and bleeding profusely. Silver emerged from the smoke with a few valiant steps, blood dripping from his neck and right shoulderblade with even more draining from deep gashes on his hip and back legs. The black and rust Doberman stumbled awkwardly with a few side steps until regaining his posture, only to take a few more steps forward and then collapse to the muddy waters in the road.

Finally I snapped out of it as the automatic cannon ripped up the roadside past me, cleaving a nearby Marine's head off his shoulders just as I hit the ground flat. Blood and brain matter burst no more than a few feet away from me, spraying warm red mist against the side of my face and helmet. My ears ached as the sounds of war buzzed in my head, stinging my hearing with a high pitched ringing and a feeling of dizzying nausea. After falling to the ground next to my dog, I clutched at Cerberus pulling him low and closer, still witnessing the carnage unfold all while feeling warm blood trickle down my face and gear. I frantically felt my neck and face for wounds, and then brushed at my shoulder, pushing a fragment of skull off me, bloody scalp and hair still attached. I looked at the men around me, lying prone in the bloody waters and then at Cerberus as he looked back to me. I tried to get a grip, and hollered to anyone that could still hear, 'Get into the jungle, now! The jungle!! Go, go!'

As we all ducked down on the road, a Marine a short distance away screamed at me, but all I could hear was the constant high pitched ringing as his mouth moved. I pointed at my ear, leading the soldier to crawl over to me and scream inches from my head, 'The Japs are heavy in the jungle on our flank, Sir.'

I yelled back at him as I unclipped Cerberus's leash and pulled a grenade from my belt, 'We are exposed in this road. Better off with cover fighting Hetai than sitting out here in the open with that flak cannon raging.' I pulled the pin and tossed my MK2 pineapple grenade as hard as I could towards the wall of dense foliage and overgrown grass, and hand signaled for my squad behind me to move towards the Japanese held forest on our flank just as the frag grenade exploded in the jungle, hopefully clearing us a path. I motioned for Cerberus to move and shouted back at the Marine, 'And let that last tank know it's got to get to the jungle, it's a sitting duck right now out here. We all are. Come on, go, go, go! Let's go men, off the road! Get to the jungle!'

We rushed to the forest, diving into the vegetation and disappearing into cover from the Hetai's sights as the rest of our Company began following suit. It was obvious we stood no chance at all out in the open, the Japanese Army was too well organized, and we marched foolishly right into their inimical and consuming trap. Now G Company was in a battle for all out survival, and against an array of devastating Imperial weaponry, not to mention the enemy held high ground. Luckily for me, Cerberus was a powerful weapon in and of himself, an he was all too well accustomed to the hell of combat, already moving us through the river grass and to a protected area as we regrouped in a profuse grove of Indian Almond trees. The battle began to erupt all around us as the Marines began engaging the IJA filled jungle in every direction. I checked to make sure my squad was intact, taking note of Pepper and her messenger unit handlers Sergeant Dunlap and Private First Class Gallo. I checked on the other Privates, Gonzales was fine, but Medic Smithers was already at hectic work on Murphy who had shrapnel lacerations on his thigh and chest, mud and blood stained most of his tattered uniform. Then I asked Jones, 'Where's Egan, Fredette, and Hall?'

Jones answered with wide eyes, his voice shaking and looking scared as shit, 'I seen Hall get taken out, Sir. I think Egan and Fredette got scattered in the mayhem.'

Murphy exclaimed through pained breaths, 'Where, in the, hell, are them Nips, hittin, us from, and with, what? That ain't, regular, artillery.' He winced as Smithers pressed Sulfa powder into his wounds to help fight any bacterial infections or tropical maladies.

'It's not coming from this hill.' I said, still waiting for my hearing to adjust, my hands had nearly stopped shaking. I continued as I pointed northeast, 'I think it's a automatic flak cannon, from the hill just north of us.'

Dunlap asked, 'You mean they're using anti-aircraft weapons against infantry?'

I replied, 'Yea seems like it, 20 mm more than likely, definitely HE shells.' Then I commanded, 'Hey Murphy, can you get us a direct line of communication with our last Sherman?' Just as I finished my request, Cerberus snapped his head to the right at full attention. We all raised our weapons frantically to where the black Doberman pointed his wedge shaped head until a Japanese infantryman sprinted into view between the trees, only to get lit up by about five soldiers before he ever knew what happened.

Gunfire volleys were being exchanged all about the jungle, and we could be hit by friendly fire just as easy as enemy bullets in this chaos. I told the men to form a defensive position while I slapped in a full en bloc, and then climbed one of the tall Indian Almond trees that rose high above the rest of the canopy. I could see complete turmoil beneath me, it's just what the IJA had wanted, luring us into irregular combat in the rainforest with their potent AA gun raining down terror on our entire Company. From nearly the highest branch, I stared through my M73 scope but couldn't make out much of the weapon, just some flashes here and there from the crest. I worked my way back down the deciduous tree to my waiting squad, with Gallo asking, 'Sir, what's going on, can you locate the AA gun?'

I answered, 'Not really, they got it camoed as hell up there, might even be in a pillbox or some extensive trench system. We are going to have to close the gap. Murphy, you alright to continue fighting?'

Smithers answered for him, 'He's stable for now, but shouldn't be doing too much moving. He might have some internal bleeding in his lungs, he's in rough shape, Sir.'

I nodded as Murphy informed me, holding his radio in one hand and pressing his other hand on his bandaged chest, 'Corporal, I can't, get a, transmission out, on my radio, nothing, but static in, this valley.. The jungle, is too thick. Interference..'

I told him, 'Thats okay Murph, just catch your breath soldier.' I looked around my exhausted squad, and continued, 'Alright, listen up men, we can still get contact with that tank. I need someone to escort Sergeant Dunlap and Murphy to the M4 Sherman, and I want Cerberus to lead Pepper and Gallo, and the rest of us, up close enough to give coordinates on this AA battery… Can Pepper get back to you with the message?'

Dunlap exclaimed, 'She can smell me more than a mile away, just find that cannon and Pepper will handle it from there.' I looked appreciatively at the little blue Doberman as she panted looking back up at me unblinkingly with big, determined, golden eyes.

Gonzales spoke up, 'Sir, I can do it, I will escort the Sergeant and Murphy to the tank.' I thanked Gonzales as he lifted up his injured brother while Murphy put his arm around Gonzales' neck and Dunlap led them back southwest. The squad split up and we started moving in the opposite direction, with Cerberus leading me through the bush and uphill, with Pepper, Gallo, Smithers, and Jones not far behind.

We trekked hard north east, quick as possible to get out of the concentrated gun battles. My Doberman wove between the Palmetto groves as we pushed back the thickets of Cycads and Tangen Tangen, and unwound the tangling vines from our arms and legs as we trailed the Scout dog. Abruptly, the trees not much more than twenty feet on our right were chopped down by the anti-aircraft gun as the rainforest was clear-cut by the large rapid fire projectiles. The four of us and our dogs hit the soggy, leaf covered, dirt as tree trunks shattered into a thousand splinters, branches crashed down from above, and leaves flew in all directions as the massive buzzsaw of destruction worked it's way past us to the south. We waited a minute to see if the exploratory fire would come back our way, and while we waited, Smithers whispered, 'So any ideas on what we are up against Corporal?'

I crawled up to a tree to place my back against and shrugged while I began to pet Cerberus, and then Pepper as Gallo brought her over. 'To be honest,' I said, 'my best guess would be a Type 98 AA 20 mm machine cannon. Japs got quite a few of them pieces. But that's only a guess.'

Pepper licked my face and nuzzled me as Cerberus sniffed at her butt, and Jones asked, 'Do you think our tank is still operational?'

I answered matter of factly, 'More than likely... I don't think that last strafing round was directed by their scouts, too messy. It looks like that auto cannon is looking for our last tank and doesn't give a shit if it hits their own troops in the process.' A few seconds later, I set Cerberus back to work as we started climbing the base of the northern hill. We parted the giant ferns and mulberry bushes, slid behind moss covered boulders, and crept through the endless array of thorny brush, Banana Palms, and breadfruit trees. There were random rows of punji stakes covered in bushy weeds and loose leaves, the deadly spikes jutting out from the incline. Their points were honed deadly sharp and just waiting to impale the shins and knees of wary soldiers too fatigued to take notice or those moving too anxiously forward in the panic of battle. However Cerberus moved us around these forest entrapments every time, his bandages were no longer wrapped around him, the guaze and tape long scraped off by the dense flora that we were submerged in and exposing his scarred gunshot wound. The Doberman pushed on through the rain, his head pivoting and his large nose inhaling, and after a few more minutes, Cerberus motioned to Hetai hidden to our left. I halted the men behind us with a flat hand, and then pointed down as the three Marines and Pepper jumped quietly to the ground.

I dropped to one knee and positioned myself behind a Banyan tree, leaning around with my M1 Garand and inspecting the situation. My war dog glared high to his left, and within a minute I sensed his focus was entirely on a tall Palm tree a couple hundred feet up the hill on our nine. I called Cerberus back to better cover and clicked the elevation knob on the scope four clicks, before leaning back around the tree to interpret visually what Cerberus already knew through his exquisite sense of smell. I scanned up the thin trunk to the proliferation of fronds at the top, with my cross hairs searching for a glimpse. Then as a gust of wind swayed the fronds to the south, in that split second it exposed two camouflaged guerillas perched in the crown of the Palm. I pulled on the trigger just enough to feel the cold steel begin to give, and placed the cross hairs on the head of the Infantryman holding a Type 99 LMG. I pulled back on the trigger just a little more as the wind died down and the fronds withdrew back to their natural position with the northern gusts, covering both the Hetai once again in leafy vegetation. It didn't matter anymore, my mind had burned the image in my eyes of their exact location, and I confidently squeezed all the way through as the M1 blasted against my shoulder and a second later a Japanese soldier fell twenty five feet from his nest, smacking hard into the ground on his back. Within the next second I had already swiveled my Garand on to the space in the tree where I knew his comrade had occupied, and blasted another Springfield round through the leaves without hesitation. Nothing happened, and I could only watch, wondering if I had missed my shot, waiting to see if any bullets would be returned in my direction. A few more seconds passed, until finally a Carbine rifle fell from the tree, followed shortly after by the second soldier as he tumbled down head over heels and soaked in blood, slamming into the mud face first.

With that threat neutralized, we were right back to climbing up the small but steep foothill, probing the incline for the dreaded weapon system that wreaked havoc over the battlefield. There were squads of Japanese soldiers making their way down the hill in a hurry on their way to support the IJA garrison as they continued the deadly assault on our overwhelmed Golf Company. Cerberus smelled the encroaching enemy forces at hundred yard distances everytime, allowing us to avoid their patrols while we infiltrated deep past their lines up the elevation. As we closed in on the crest, small rocks fell past us as the flak gun roared above, trembling the hillside as it tore up the battle zone below without mercy. I stopped our squad's advance, knowing we couldn't get much closer without being discovered, and showered Cerberus in praise for a few seconds while our men gathered close to us behind a fallen tree. I located a climbable Ifit tree nearby and started to scale the deciduous hardwood, with the sole purpose to find the bunker and gain the coordinates for our big guns. At about 70 feet high in the Ifit just above the canopy, I kept my M1 slung around my shoulder and scanned the crest through my scope. I withdrew a damp military map from my pocket and scoured the groves of Coconut palms and Ifit trees that adorned the precipice, searching in vain for the murder hole from which the IJA rained terror down on our Company. I scanned and scanned until finally the auto cannon sounded off again, slamming the valley with 20 mm high velocity HE shells. The muzzle flash and thundering blast helped me lock on to the bunker, a skillfully concealed Kamekobaka or "turtle-back tomb" pillbox made of quarried stone, and this one with a couple feet of reinforced concrete and iron rebar. The hulking bunker was probably fronting a cave system that led back to Tenjo Mountain, and had multiple loop holes on both sides with several daunting Type 92 7.7 mm Shiki Kikanju HMGs peering out on its flanks, allowing the pillbox to have virtually no weak points. It was a hell of a little fortress, with trees and bushes planted all around it to camouflage the tomb from both the air and land. At front and center was a murder hole with a set of 5 foot twin barrels sticking out over the river basin. I realized I was only half right, as I witnessed the weapon system the IJA were using was actually a Type 4 Twin 20 mm Anti Aircraft gun. The Type 4 was actually a product of combining two Type 98 20 mm flak guns into a single 1 ton monster, equipped with two giant 20 round box clips and a gas operated system that was capable of shooting over 3 miles in range with a 2 mile high ceiling, and at a rate of 600 explosive rounds per minute.

I kept glancing back down at my map, knowing I couldn't just estimate these coordinates, because if the M4 medium tank was going to strike back, than the Sherman would have to expose itself to the wrath of the Type 4 Twin 20 mm machine cannon. This meant any misses or miscalculations on our side would more than probably end in the immediate destruction of our last Sherman tank, as I was sure the Imperial Japanese Army had pre-sighted the entire valley for such an opportunity. I balanced precariously from the Ifit branches as I removed a protractor from my coat, and began calculating the 1:25,000 scale grid map to the best of my ability, trying desperately to pinpoint that Type 4 Twin as it rocketed down shells into the gully.

Finally as sure as I was going to be, I wrote down the set of coordinates and dropped down the tree as fast as I could. Gallo quickly took the map from me and looked at the points I had jotted as he read the coordinates, asking me, 'You sure about this Sir?'

I replied, 'Yea, I think so… I mean my calculations look right.' Gallo nodded and jotted down the grid coordinates in code on a small notepad, ripped the page out, folded it and placed the invaluable knowledge within a compartment in Pepper's specialized collar.

The beautiful blue girl's eyes focused with an intensity only seen in the Doberman Pinscher, and with a command from her handler and a slap on her shoulder, the greyish blue canine sprinted down the hillside as her long uncropped ears bounced in the wind until she vanished into the rainforest. We crouched around the fallen Ifit tree, apprehensive to what troubles awaited Pepper as she ran the message back to Sergeant Dunlap. I could see the valley lighting up with machine gun fire, explosions pocked the beautiful forest, leveling trees flat and leaving plumes of black smoke all over the jungle. I could also see the foreboding concern on Gallo's face, it was obvious he was worried about Pepper as she traversed the intensifying combat being waged in the river valley.

I looked through my M73 scope at the escalating battle, it appeared that G Company and the IJA had reformed more conventional battle lines in the jungle, which wasn't in out favor as long as the enemy held the artillery advantage. I recognized that the Type 4 Twin 20 mm strafing fire was more targeted now, no doubt being directed by the Japanese field scouts to our Marines' whereabouts in the tropical forest. I just prayed that Gonzales and Dunlap had found our last Sherman tank, and even more that the Sherman was still operational as it definitely got hit in the initial assault. I trusted that if Dunlap and Gonzales did their job, then Pepper would find them with our coded message and we could still turn the tide before it was too late. Surprisingly I located Pepper as she flew out of some Palm groves and through a meadow of tall grass just as the Hetai in the forest edge also took notice. The treeline erupted with a combination of Type 100 SMGs, Type 4 Japanese Garands, and Type 38 and Type 97 Arisaka bolt action rifles, the ravenous foot soldiers desperate to kill Pepper and stop her invaluable message as she wove through the field with bullets ripping up the ground just behind her. She sprinted under a collapsed tree with machinegun fire riddling the log with holes, showering her in wood chips as she squeezed under it just in time, and then jumped another log before bounding over a small stream bed. The athletic Doberman soared over the obstacles with yet even more bullets skimming the heroic dog as the IJA emptied their clips on her. Pepper dashed like a blur several more yards through the river grass as a Japanese Type 97 hand grenade exploded not far behind her. She was just able to escape the muddy blast radius as Pepper hurdled herself over a soldier's dead body and out of the grenade smoke and back into the woods, out of danger momentarily.

I trained my rifle on the Infantryman that Pepper had drawn furthest out of the treeline and centered my sights on his chest. I reset the elevation knob, and adjusted the windage a few clicks to accommodate my bullet strike to the steady, northeastern, gales. Before he could retreat back to the forest, I let the Garand deliver a .30-06 Springfield through the shocked Hetai's sternum, blowing chunks of his heart and lungs out of his back and onto the grassy meadow. As he fell into the reeds next to the shallow stream, the rest of his squad retreated back into the trees trying to figure out where the Sniper round had originated from. I continued to train my M1's scope across the battlefield, trying to find Pepper and see if I could offer her any cover fire as she courageously galloped on. Jones asked me, 'Do you see her Corporal?' I didn't answer, the Twin 20 mm roared just over our heads and continued pummeling our Company's positions unceasingly. I knew we were running out of time.

A few moments later, Gallo spoke up as he spotted his Messenger dog through his binoculars in a thinned section of jungle where the 20 mm AA gun had cut paths of destruction through the terrain. Sure enough, I too found Pepper dashing left and right around the broken tree trunks and splintered brush. A Japanese foot soldier popped up from a spider hole and busted a Light Machinegun off at the blue girl as she traversed the war torn forest with great leaps and bounds, small arms fire tearing into trees all around her as she raced onward. Pepper dove head first through a thicket of brush with 8mm automatic Nambu rounds following her and randomly sprayed the thickets, the blue Doberman courageously refused to quit no matter the deadly deterrences that faced her. She dashed the last remaining yards to her second handler Dunlap, with her claws digging desperately into the ground for traction, her movements fluid and majestic, her singular goal all consuming. She came to a skidding stop at Dunlap's feet, and the exuberant Sergeant bent down to greet his heroic Doberman and withdrew the encrypted message from her collar while Gonzales let off some cover fire for the war dog unit with his M1 Garand. Dunlap at once unfolded the code, ignoring the battle around them and deciphered the coordinates while he quickly picked up the telephone on the back of the M4 Sherman, speaking through the several inches of steel armor via the direct phone line to Tank Commander Hanchett, relaying him our desperate message. As luck would have it, the last Sherman was an upgraded M4A1 model, with a replaced turret that held a 76 mm tank gun instead of the standard 75 mm. Although the extra millimeter added to the bore made almost no difference, it was the extended shell of the 76 mm which held much more propellant and allowed for a more powerful weapon with far greater velocity and a better designed armor penetrating shell would prove vital to knocking out that Type 4 Twin autocannon behind its protected bunker. We probably won't get another chance I thought as Sergeant Dunlap finished his communication, hanging up the phone and falling back into the rainforest with faithful Pepper right at his side.

The M4A1 Sherman suddenly started crashing through the small trees and plunged out into the flooded road again, in clear view of the 20 mm Flak gun. The ten foot tall, 84,000 lbs tank rolled through the muddy waters with several punctures in its side hull and holding some sand bags and spare track links welded to its front for extra protection. The five man crew consisted of a gunner, shell loader, driver, assistant driver who was also the bow gunner, and the Tank Commander. The entire crew's lives depended on the chemistry they had developed as Commander Hanchett put them right out in the open in a last ditch effort to draw first blood with the IJA pill box. The tank spun it's tracks at 25 mph until it shifted down and then to a complete stop as the 76 mm gun raised its angle of trajectory and the turret pivoted on target. It all hinged on the intelligence my squad gathered and whether the tank crew was capable of sighting in those coordinates quickly enough. Smithers watched over my shoulder through his binoculars, speaking more to himself than anyone, 'We got one shot at this'.

I whispered back gruffly, 'Let's make it count god damn it.' Just then, the swampy earth imploded in gun shot after gun shot as the automatic 20 mm cannon strafed up the road towards the Sherman. Then the M4A1(76) Sherman tank gun flared as it discharged an (AP) Armor Piercing M62A1 HE 15.43 lbs projectile at 2,700 feet per second towards the calculated position on the crest. The path of exploding mud in the road stalled just feet from the tank as we all held our breath. The M62A1 shell had struck true, rupturing the Kamekobaka bunker with the APCBC round breaking through the three foot thick walls and detonating its TNT core inside the pill box. The entire IJA bunker was filled with the Sherman's fury as steel shards were hurled in every direction, fatally slicing bodies apart and warping the notorious Type 4 Twin 20 mm automatic cannon into scrap metal. Staff Sergeant Hanchett ordered another shot at once, as the loader lifted the 25 lbs shell into the chamber feeding the massive gun, and the tank gunner pulled the trigger, recoiling the whole tank with the rain shuddering off the barrel as another deadly M62A1 shell punctured the fortified tomb walls and shredded the bunker from the inside out as plumes of smoke poured out from the loopholes.

The reinforced Kamekobaka bunker was devastated, as Commander Hanchett blasted the blockhouse one more time for good measure before turning his Sherman medium tank back on the Hetai filled jungle with the side armament .50 cal Browning M2HB blazing into the lines of Japanese infantry. The IJA blasted back harmlessly at the tank with their small arms fire bouncing off the armor in sparks as the Sherman took full control of the battlefield. With the fall of the 20 mm machine cannon that had brutally ruled the battlefield, our Marines finally stood a fighting chance. Our lines reorganized behind our M4A1 medium tank and our greater numbers began to flank our foes from the West, and with the river trapping them on the East, the fighting slowly diminished as the Imperial Japanese garrison was forced to retreat up the hills and towards their cave systems. As Cerberus led us back down the hill and out of enemy territory to rally with our brothers, I realized the vital Intel our squad had gained behind enemy lines had saved our entire Company.

Once we got back to friendly lines, we got word that Foxtrot Company was already sending reinforcements from Smoky Ridge to bolster our efforts. I reformed my squad, and found Pepper with Dunlap, Gonzales, and Murphy. The rambunctious blue Doberman ran up to me and Cerberus, and I bent to one knee and enveloped the war dog in a strong hug as she kissed my cheek with her tail wagging wildly. I knew there was still more fighting to do to secure the valley, but I took a second to enjoy the moment, especially I thought, when every moment could be the very last. With gunshots still ringing in the forest just beyond, Pepper's big puppy eyes looked into mine as I stroked her ear, and told her, 'You saved the mission girl, you saved us.. You saved the entire Company girl.'

Acknowledgements

Exactly 1,047 dogs had trained as Marine Devil Dogs during World War II, and the Army trained an additional 3,000 war dogs. During the battles, the dogs led the points for infantry on advances, explored caves, pill boxes, dugouts, and scouted fortified positions. They worked sentry duty with military police at crossroads day and night. They occupied foxholes with the Marines and Army alike in forward outposts at night. Early on, in the Dutch East Indies, the 31st Division used the 26th QM War Dog Platoon to help conduct 250 patrols in the course of two-and-a-half months. In this period, not a single one of these patrols was ambushed, proving the invaluable nature of the scout dogs who could alert soldiers to the presence of the enemy at distances ranging from seventy to 200 yards away, every time. By the time the U.S. invaded the IJA held Philippines, there was not enough dog units to go around, as every infantry patrol was requesting a Scout dog be attached. Often, the advanced warning of the scout dogs enabled GIs to reverse the odds and surprise Japanese foot soldiers.

These Devil Dogs and their handlers were officially credited with leading over three hundred and fifty patrols in Guam alone, during the mop up phases of the battles. The handlers accounted for over three hundred enemy Japanese slain, with only one handler killed on patrol. The dogs were invaluable in the jungle warfare that characterized much of the combat in the Pacific Theater. The impenetrable jungle limited human effectiveness, reliant on eyesight and hearing, but the dogs could smell the presence of the enemy despite the obstacles.

Both dogs and handlers provided an invaluable contribution to the American war effort in World War II. Despite the almost constant peril and close combat experienced by scout dog and messenger dog platoons, history has almost forgotten these heros of liberty in the darkest of times. Though man and beast alike may not have received the credit they deserved during the war, they proved their worth and pioneered many new tactics. Their legacy can still be found in the military working dogs of the modern Military.

Rolo was one of the first to join the Devil Dogs, and unfortunately was the first Marine dog to be killed in action. 29 war dogs were listed as killed in action, with 25 of those deaths occurring on the island of Guam. The U.S. Marine Core maintains a War Memorial established by former 1st Lt. William W. Putney, who was the veterinarian for the dogs on Guam. The monument for those 25 fallen War Dogs stands iconically for the breed. Here are some of these heroic canine's daring accomplishments.

War Dog Cemetery, Guam 1944. USMC Photo

The Devil Dogs

Andy

"The most outstanding incident of record for the First Marine Dog Platoon on Bougainville, came on November 14, with Andy (a Dobe) and his handlers as the principals. Andy was the Doberman who had led the Raiders inland on the D-day: he was popularly referred to as "Gentleman Jim" because of his aristocratic demeanor and aloofness with the other dogs.

A Marine force up front ran into stiff Jap resistance that day of the action. Andy's two handlers, Privates Robert E. Lansley and John B. Mahoney, volunteered to take their

Dobermans and seek out the enemy strong points.

Andy With One Of His Handlers,
Private John B. Mahoney, Bougainville.

They had complete faith in Andy's ability to spot whatever was out there. The three moved beyond the lines into the heavy foliage. Andy was about 25 yards out front, when he stopped short; and looked to the left and right, the way he always alerted. The two soldiers crept up along a little trail behind Andy and saw two machine gun nests, one of each side of the trail. The two handlers started shooting, Lansley threw two grenades and when it was all over, eight Japs were dead. The wiping out of the machine gun nests by Andy and the two handlers permitted that entire sector of the line to move forward."

Buster

"Brand Number A684: While operating as a messenger dog with "F" Company 155th Infantry Regiment on Morotai Island, Buster was directly responsible for saving the lives of an entire patrol consisting of seventeen men.

His determined effort carried him through heavy enemy machine gun and mortar fire on a total of two trips, bringing instructions for the patrol to hold its position at all costs. He was thus responsible for reinforcements which accounted for the destruction of an entire enemy force."

Jack

"On D plus 7 days, as the Raiders pushed on into the jungle, Jack, a German Shepherd messager dog, and one of his handlers were hit during a sharp fire fight. Despite receiving a deep gash across his back, Jack reached his other handler with a message that the Nips had struck and stretcher bearers were needed. With the phone lines cut, Jack was the only means of communications the advance party had that day."

Bruce

"Brand Number T178: During a banzai attack occurring in Northern Luzon at 0315 hours on February 17th, 1945 against "E" Company 27th Infantry. Bruce without command voluntarily attacked three Japanese infantrymen advancing with fixed bayonets towards a foxhole containing two wounded American soldiers. By his fearless action the lives of the two wounded men were saved; by discouraging the advance of these particular Japanese, more casualties were averted."

Chips

"On the Sicily beachhead, the tired soldiers who had slogged ashore with Chips stopped for a breather when they found shelter, they thought, behind a ruined pillbox. In violation of the cardinal rule of his K-9 training, Chips broke away from his handler and ran away. The men found out the reason for this outrageous breach of etiquette a moment later when one of the Germans' dreaded MG-42 machine guns opened up on them. The gun, however, quit firing momentarily before it could inflict any casualties. Advancing on the machine-gun nest, the GIs found Chips, despite a bullet wound received in his charge, holding down the German gunner by his throat and thus "encouraging" the surrender of the rest of the gun crew."

Blackie

"Brand Number H24: On 12 and 13 April 1945 while on a two day-patrol with Company F, 123rd Infantry, Blackie, handled by Corporal Technician Kido, was used alternately on the point.

The patrol successfully completed its mission without detection by the enemy, locating an area where 500 Japanese were bivouacked. As patrol was on reconnaissance, all contact with the enemy was avoided."

Dick

"A scout dog donated by Edward Zan of New York City, was cited for working with a Marine Corps patrol in the Pacific Area. This dog not only discovered a camouflaged Japanese bivouac but unerringly alerted to the only occupied hut of five, permitting a surprise attack which resulted in annihilation of the enemy with a single Marine casualty."

Caesar

"Bougainville: Mayo and Caesar led a Marine company on a mission to prevent the enemy from penetrating the command post area. Radio communications were of no use in the thick jungle; Caesar was the only form of communication. Nine times the dog was dispatched with vital information back-and-forth between the two handlers, always under heavy fire.

On the second day of the mission, the dog team was sleeping when Caesar heard a sound which woke him. Mayo reacted to the movement of his dog in time to see a hand grenade drop at their feet. The soldier was able to throw the device back in the direction it came from, where it exploded. The next morning eight Japanese bodies were discovered where Mayo had hurled the grenade.

The third day of this encounter was nearly the last day of Caesar's life. The enemy tried again to sneak in on the MWD team position. Mayo didn't realize it, but Caesar did. Although he wasn't trained to attack, the dog leaped at the Japanese soldiers in defense of Mayo. The handler called the dog back to his position. As the dog returned, he was shot twice.

One shot lodged deep behind his left shoulder after entering the left hind leg. The bullet was close to Caesar's heart and Lt. Commander Steven L. Steigler, the Raider Regimental surgeon, decided it would be too risky to try to remove it. Caesar carried that chunk of lead for the rest of his life.

Note: Caesar was credited with carrying the first war dog message of the war in actual combat. He was one of four dogs injured on Bougainville."

Danny

"When an assault patrol was given the mission of locating and destroying an enemy machine gun nest, Sergeant Knisely and his scout dog, Danny, took the point. Twice the dog alerted, and scouts went forward but were unable to spot the well hidden nest. Then the handler volunteered to lead the patrol as close as possible. Slowly and cautiously they moved up. Danny alerted very strongly, and the sergeant pointed out the gun's exact position. But in the fight that eliminated it and its crew, Knisely was killed. He was awarded the Silver Star posthumously."

Wolf

"Wolf was leading an infantry patrol through the Corabello Mountains toward the strategic Belete Pass, when he scented a Jap party entrenched on a hill about one hundred and fifty yards distant. The patrol launched a surprise attack. In the hot engagement that followed, Wolf was severely wounded by shell fragments. Since he never whimpered or showed signs of pain, the men around him failed to notice that he had been hit. As the firing increased in intensity, the Americans realized they were heavily outnumbered and were being encircled. Again the dog, and his handler took post at the point. Three times Wolf's alerts enabled the patrol to avoid Jap columns closing in on it. Wounded though he was, Wolf finally guided the American troops out of the trap and back to their command post. When the gallant animal's wounds were discovered, an emergency operation was performed but could not save him."

Duchess

"Doberman Pinscher Duchess, brand #7H74: was a prized member of the 39th Infantry Scout Dog Platoon. On April 30th, 1945 Duchess handled by Sgt. Knight, on patrol with the 3rd Battalion, 123rd Infantry, was used in the inspection of enemy cave installations on Luzon in the Philippines. On approaching a large one, the dog was permitted to go to the entrance. At this point she gave a strong alert. Grenades were thrown into the cave, after which the patrol moved on. Investigation the following day revealed 33 Japanese dead in the cave.

On another occasion Duchess and Sgt. Knight were on patrol with the same unit. Duchess alerted on some Filipino huts, 800 yards away. Closer investigation of the patrol disclosed the presence of the Japs. Mortar and machine-gun fire were used to kill 9 Japanese soldiers in the hut."

*All Accomplishments are quoted and cited from: https://www.k9history.com/WWII-uscm-devil-dogs.htm

Printed in Great Britain
by Amazon